HELLFIRE
&
DAMNATION
III

HELLFIRE & DAMNATION III

Connie Corcoran Wilson

2014

Hellfire & Damnation III

© 2015 Connie Corcoran Wilson

Quad City Press

Cover art by Vincent Chong

Layout and design by John Teehan

Published in the USA

ISBN—978-0-98244-487-0

Table of Contents

Introduction

This collection of stories, third in the ***HELLFIRE & DAMNATION*** series, is connected thematically by Dante's "Inferno." You will travel through stories representing Dante's nine Circles of Hell and the crimes or sins punished at each of those nine Circles of Hell.

Circle One: Limbo
Circle Two: Lust
Circle Three: Gluttony
Circle Four: Avarice & Prodigality
Circle Five: Wrath, Sullenness
Circle Six: Heresy
Circle Seven: The Violent
Circle Eight: The Fraudulent
Circle Nine: Treachery

As William F. Nolan, author of "Logan's Run" and "Nightworlds" and a Living Legend in Dark Fantasy said of *Hellfire & Damnation I*:

"Let me start right off by saying that Connie Wilson presents what I call 'matter-of-fact' horror. She writes solid, declarative sentences rife with dark undertones. No fancy description for Connie. No sentimental musings. No soft emotionalism. Just hard-edged documentary style storytelling. Jolting objective sentences made all the more disturbing by their cool directness. Frankly—and I consider myself well-read in the shock genre—I have never encountered a style such as she displays here, in story after story. Connie Wilson's dark talent is unique, and readers will stagger away from her icy tales, stunned and groggy.

Her frame for this collection is also unique: stories built around Dante's nine Circles of Hell. A unifying concept that is classically fresh... Once you read this remarkably fresh collection, you'll emerge with some twisted new thoughts...

Believe me, Dear Reader, you've never encountered anything like "Hellfire & Damnation," the series. I have a final word for it: *WOW!*

Circle One: Limbo

The Cave Robber

Dark, profound it was, and cloudy, so that though I fixed my
sight on the bottom I did not discern anything there.
– *Canto IV, Dante's Inferno*

"I swear! Something pulled on it! Something pulled it down! I swear!"
Josh was hot, sweaty and disheveled. He rubbed his hands together,
twisting his interlocked knuckles tightly where, only moments before, they
were clutching the thick rope, preparing to drop it into the mouth of the
cave. Spelunking in the Pacific Northwest was a first for the thirteen-year-
old boy. Now he'd dropped the only rope the three boys had secured for
their Saturday afternoon adventure.

"Nice going, Nitwit!" Blake Norton was not amused.

Blake swiped the rope from his father's supply of ropes and ladders
(and other assorted paraphernalia) in the workshop behind the Nortons'
small frame house. His father referred to this collection of random objects
on shelves alongside their two cars as "the garage." It was more workshop
than garage, containing, as Blake so eloquently put it, "all kinds of crap."
Blake wasn't in the mood to get caught stealing one of dear old Dad's ropes.
Or ladders. Or tools.

"Shit! If my dad finds out I took one of his precious ropes, he'll take it
out on me, Numbnuts! Why didn't you hang on tighter?"

Josh glanced at Blake and then inspected his reddened hands. No cal-
louses there. Josh was used to pushing a pencil, not hauling ropes. His scuffed
fingers hurt like hell. The acrid odor of sweat and blood filled his nostrils.

"I *WAS* holding onto it, Blake. Honest!"

The pleading tone in Josh's voice was enough to convince the third member of the group, Nate Sullivan, that Josh Wells was telling the truth. Josh *was* very sorry the rope was gone. Nate always ended up playing mediator between alpha male Blake and his less testosterone-laden buddies.

Looks like another job for the Mediator, thought Nate. Silent tribute to Arnold Schwarzenegger's iconic film.

Josh ranked at the bottom of the Terrible Trio. Usually, Blake and Nate hung out with more athletic, more popular 8th grade boys.

Josh is really a dweeb, Nate thought , watching the pudgy boy rub his hands together while grimacing in pain. Josh peered into the mouth of the cave. Massaged his injured hands. A remorseful expression signaled sincerity. Josh might not be macho, but over the summer he'd earned his Eagle Scout Badge. He knew about "tying knots and shit," as Blake called it. That was the reason Josh was invited to help the others explore the cave.

The cave was located deep within the coastal forests that ran from California to British Columbia. The nearest town was Clampton, California. Blake called it "Poopyville." There wasn't much to do in a logging town with a population of one thousand people. The nearby primeval forests were the only escape and diversion.

Blake and his buddies discovered the cave while playing paintball. When he first found the deep-set well-concealed opening to the underground cavern, Blake thought, *Someday, I'll go spelunking in that cave. Find out what's down there.*

Today was that some day. Blake contacted the two friends for the Saturday afternoon adventure, stole the rope from his father's workbench, bought three flashlights at George Graham's hardware/convenience store in tiny Clampton, and told the others to bring a knapsack and a water canteen. The trio set off on an adventure. On this foggy Saturday morning, surrounded by giant redwoods and the eerie cries of birds and small animals, Jake was determined to find out what was at the bottom of Norton's Cave. Blake declared that, since he had found it, the cave should be named for him. Typical.

Nate thought, *Why did you give the rope to Josh in the first place? Josh is a screw-up!* He moved to intervene between the always-impetuous Blake and the less aggressive Josh.

Josh was still protesting loudly, red palms displayed for all to see. "I was holding on to it real tight. Look! Really—I was. Something pulled on it. I swear!"

Blake regarded him coldly. A hostile, dispassionate look.

Nate, in a placating tone of voice, offered alternative scenarios.

"It's okay, Josh. Any one of us could have dropped the rope. We'll just get another one."

As he said that, Nate shrugged, as though finding a twenty-foot sturdy hemp rope that would support Blake, a boy who weighed as much as most men, would be as easy as picking up a pack of chewing gum.

Blake snorted derisively. "HA! Obviously, you guys don't know my dad very well. If he thought I took THAT rope, he'd tan my hide!"

"My dad has a rope ladder—from when we used to have a boat," said Nate. "It's not as long as your rope was, though, Blake."

"How long is it?" Blake sounded irritated.

"Fifteen feet?"

"Are you sure?"

"I don't know exactly. I think so." The indecisive look on his face gave away Nate's uncertainty. "My dad thought we were going to get invited to use this big yacht that he *says* his best friend in the Bahamas owns." Nate's expression changed to crestfallen. "That never happened."

Nate's dad was always full of big talk. Always making plans which seldom panned out.

"We need to make sure that it's plenty long enough. Just make sure this one you say you can get is going to get us all the way down and back. We'll try again tomorrow."

Blake stalked off towards the trampled pathway that led from the woods, walking briskly. His impatience with both Nate and Josh was clear.

As the duo followed Blake, trudging away from the yawning maw of the subterranean cave entrance, Blake looked back at Josh and said, "And YOU'RE not touching the rope next time, Shit-for-brains. Got it? You'll be the last one down. In fact, let's see if Kitra Moon will join us tomorrow. She's nuts about caves. She loves crap like that."

Blake said this as though the only reason he wanted to invite the cutest girl in class to accompany them was because of her interest in spelunking. The truth was something different. Every boy in class had a crush on Kitra. She was blonde, smart, pretty and spirited.

"I can ask Kitra if she wants to go," Josh's voice began to sound hopeful. "We study together sometimes at the library." Josh hoped against hope that he might somehow redeem himself by making this offer to intercede with Kitra.

"Good idea, Josh. She'd probably say yes to you. It's the least you can do to make up for dropping my dad's rope." Blake huffed off. In the lead. Walking alone.

On Sunday, at noon, the trio of boys set off on the path leading into the woods near Clampton. Clampton Reserve was such a small part of the large naturally forested area of the state that the road through it was little more than a dirt path.

Kitra, as Blake had predicted, thought the idea of an adventure with the boys sounded fun. She'd known all three boys since kindergarten. She liked Josh and Nate. She merely tolerated Blake. Blake was abusive to his smaller, gentler peers. Kitra wasn't a fan.

"Hey, Moon-ie!" Blake greeted Kitra, as the three boys approached.

She stood there at the entrance to the forest. The dark green canopy of trees behind her contrasted with her blonde hair, which glittered like crystal in the bright sunlight of the crisp fall Sunday afternoon.

Kitra Moon's name inspired jokes. It also elicited some bullying from her California classmates. Her parents immigrated from Tibooburra, Australia. Kitra hoped the others never learned the name of her Australian hometown. Clampton wasn't the big city of L.A., where parents routinely named their children Moon Unit or Zuma.

"Don't make fun of my name, Blake." She fixed Blake with a steely gaze that promised a fight.

"Hey! I'm not making fun of your name," Blake sneered. "It's a cool name—if you're a planet."

"News flash, Blake: the moon is not a planet." Kitra silently scored one for her side.

Josh spoke. "I think your name is neat, Kitra. You're the only Kitra I know." He directed an embarrassed smile at his study buddy.

"Why, thanks, Josh." Kitra smiled.

"Me, too," added Nate.

"Me too what?" Kitra was asking Nate to explain his remark.

"I think your name is very pretty, too," Nate responded.

"Ooooh," Blake began his usual ridicule of any display of male sensitivity. In a mocking, high-pitched voice, Blake said, "Oh, Kitra. Your name is SO pretty. *YOU* are so pretty. Will you be my girlfriend?" Blake cackled. A sarcastic laugh.

Josh looked away, embarrassed. He wanted to shout, *SHUT UP, Blake*! But Josh also wanted to keep his original nose.

Nate began his usual peace-keeping duties.

"Lay off, Blake. You know what we meant. Kitra's an unusual name."

"Well, I'm an unusual girl," Kitra said, with a smile, "and to prove it, I brought these."

Kitra held out small sacks for each boy. In each sack were beef jerky sticks she'd purchased at George Graham's convenience store. She had passed the store on the path to the cave. George sold gas. Foodstuffs. Hardware. Anything in demand in Clampton.

"So, are we going to do this, or are we going to stand around discussing the difference between a planet and a star?" Blake was still annoyed by Kitra's earlier put-down.

Kitra tried to look bored. In reality, she was very excited. She'd much rather be spelunking in a cave than doing needlepoint, her mother's idea of a hobby. The rest of the girls in their small class were—well…boring.

Nate, as promised, had sneaked into his father's garage and stolen the second rope—actually a rope ladder. It was easier to climb down this ladder because it had actual steps. But the rope ladder wasn't as long as Blake's hemp rope

They secured the ladder-like rope to a nearby tree. Blake insisted that it be tied around the tree trunk and that an iron stake be driven into the ground for additional safety.

"We're not going to have another situation where the damn rope ends up on the floor of the cave. We have to get out of this cave as well as into it." Blake glared at the others.

A prophetic statement.

"No kidding?" Kitra said sarcastically, looking at Blake while exaggeratedly batting big turquoise blue eyes. She turned her attention to the matter at hand: "Who's going down first?"

"Why don't I start? I'm the lightest of the boys," said Nate, almost apologetically.

That much was true. There was no argument from Blake or Josh. Nate began the precarious climb into the depths of a cave that yawned pitch black below them. As black as night. Blacker than space. His knapsack, slung over his right shoulder, contained a flashlight, the beef jerky, and a canteen of water. Nate had also brought some matches.

About halfway into the murky depths, the ladder ended. Nate eyed the floor of the cave below. He could barely see anything as he aimed his flashlight at the area below. A dense, sinister fog obscured his view. He thought he saw a rock-free landing area. It was a good seven-foot drop. He hung onto the bottom of the rope ladder, legs dangling below him like the tail of a kite, trying to reduce the distance he'd have to drop to approximately five feet. Inwardly cursing the fact that the rope ladder would not take him all the way to the bottom. Then Nate let go.

The others heard a thud, followed by a howl of pain.

"What is it? What happened?" Kitra's Mother Hen instincts kicked in. She wanted to know what had gone wrong at the bottom of the rope ladder.

"I landed on a rock… my ankle…I think it's sprained… maybe broken." Nate's voice echoed off the walls of the cistern-like entrance to the sunken cave. He didn't even sound like himself. Suppressed tears choked his voice.

"Stay there, Buddy. I'm coming down," Blake hollered. Authoritative. Masculine. Commanding.

Blake began his descent. Courtesy of Nate's painful discovery of the rock in their way, which Nate had moved out of the way of the others, Blake's landing was unremarkable.

Josh followed. Kitra came last. Blake offered to catch the tiny blonde girl. She didn't especially want to be held in Blake Norton's arms, but she accepted the offer. Blake caught her with ease. He set Kitra on the ground beside the trio. Quickly disentangling herself from Blake's grasp, Kitra noticed what looked like bones.

"Looks like some poor animal fell down here and got killed," said Kitra. She knelt down to examine the bones more closely. Poked at the dry remains of some unfortunate creature—perhaps a small dog or a cat. The boys glanced at the skeleton, but they were more concerned with examining Nate's rapidly-swelling ankle. Nate was crouched in a corner of the cave, hugging his knee, inspecting his badly bruised ankle. He was trying hard not to moan in pain. Biting his lip. Beads of sweat stood out on his upper lip. He wanted to appear brave. He hoped to save face in front of Kitra.

"I'm not going to be able to walk on this," Nate said. " I'll have to wait here. Give me a boost up to the rope ladder. I'll climb back up and wait in the forest. This place gives me the creeps."

The cave was, indeed, creepy.

The cleared area immediately below the rope—the landing site—had two tunnels leading from it, one leading to the left, and one leading to the right. A lake-like area with stagnant water and crystalline structures, was straight ahead, stunning in the gloom. Aiming their flashlights at the lake revealed weird small silver fish swimming beneath a thick green scum. The algae glowed a preternatural shade of chartreuse in the dim light. Stalactites and stalagmites loomed in the tunnels ahead, twinkling and damp.

"We'd better get going," said Kitra. "We didn't start early enough. We don't want to be down here after dark."

"It's *your* fault we didn't start at first light," Blake reminded her. "You were the one who had to go to church first."

"You oughta' try going to church once in a while, Blake. I'm sure you have a few sins to confess. Maybe even some impure thoughts?"

Kitra knew her adversary. She saw, immediately that her last remark scored a bulls-eye.

"Yeah? Well, all I'm saying is that we have to get going. It will be dark in a couple hours."

"Norton's Cave." Kitra snorted derisively. "Is that name in honor of the Norton Anti-Virus?"

Nate and Josh laughed. Blake's face blackened like a small storm cloud.

Kitra continued, "On the 'let's get going front', Blake, no problem. Which tunnel do *you* want to take?" Kitra gestured towards the two tunnels that led away from the luminescent lake in front of them.

Blake, not wanting to appear indecisive, said, "That one," gesturing to the right.

Kitra said, "Okay. YOU take the one on the right—the one more traveled, no doubt, since most people are right-handed. You've heard about the road less traveled—right? Robert Frost? I'm left-handed. I'll take the one that goes left. Anybody want to go with me?"

Josh piped up, "I will, Kitra."

The last thing Josh wanted was to be left alone with Blake Norton to suffer more verbal abuse. At least Kitra was always nice to him.

"Okay, wusses," Blake said, "you explore the tunnel to the left. I'm going to find out what's in the tunnel to the right. Coordinate your watches. We'll meet back here in one hour. At two o'clock."

Off they went, after Blake helped boost Nate up to the bottom of the rope ladder. When the others disappeared into the two tunnels, Nate was grappling with the next rung, slowly and painfully inching his way towards daylight. "I'll be all right. You guys get started. You don't have much time."

One hour later, the trio re-convened. The bottom of the clearing. The opening to the cave floor. They walked past Blake's original rope, crumpled there. It had several cuts, as though it had been chewed or ripped apart. Had it snagged on some sharp rocks when it fell? The rope was old and shredded from wear.

The first dropped rope was a one quarter inch hemp or manila rope, good for a variety of tasks like farm work. Farmers referred to this type of rope as "the workhorse." It could hold 500 pounds. But it also would shrink if it got wet, which would be a problem with the lake so close. Josh's boat rope was a three-strand nylon rope. Unlike Blake's rope, it would not shrink when wet. It was perfect for dock lines or rope swings or climbing. It had better shock absorption. The steps—which were designed for swimmers boarding a large yacht—were just an added plus. The only problem was the rope's inadequate length. Nate had proven that the hard way. The rope was not long enough.

As they returned to the central meeting place, Kitra noticed small pieces of twine from the first hemp rope littering the floor of the tunnel. *How did these pieces of rope get here?* she thought.

When the three explorers reconvened at the landing site, the sight that greeted them was horrific. Nate lay on the floor of the cave. On his right side. Motionless. His back to the others.

"Shit!" Kitra rushed to Nate's side. "He must have fallen! We should have waited to make sure he got back out of the cave okay."

When the trio turned Nate's body from his right side to his back, blood gushed from a jagged slit in his throat.

"Did that happen in the fall?" Kitra's voice quavered. "I thought you said the rope ladder was secure?" As she asked, she looked at Blake, eyes luminous with tears. Accusing. Defiant. Blake stood nearby in queasy silence. Josh tried to hold it together, but a tear slid down his cheek. He sank to his knees. Felt Nate's wrist for a pulse. Nate's neck was a wide, bloody, gaping wound. No sign of life. His eyes were staring. Wild. Pupils dilated in death.

A closer look at the bottom half of Blake's first rope, lying nearby—the rope Josh dropped into the cave's depths on Saturday—revealed some small hope. The damaged rope might not be completely useless. A five-foot segment might be salvageable. It could be used to lengthen the nylon rope.

"Hey! The rope ladder *WAS* secure," Blake answered, his voice surly. "I have no idea how Nate managed to fall off the ladder. The top part of the rope is still in place. Thank God for that! It's too short. Nate fell because the replacement rope he provided wasn't long enough. Don't blame me! We're going to have to re-attach this part (*Blake indicated the usable five-foot portion on the ground*). We can connect the two pieces. Old tied to new. Lengthen the nylon boat rope. I don't know what-the-hell happened. But we're going to be in a world of hurt unless we can get that rope ladder reconnected and get out of here."

Blake was worried. It showed.

A cursory examination of the lifeless form of their friend brought more tears from tender-hearted Josh. Kitra kept moaning, "Poor Nate! Poor Nate!"

Blake looked ill-at-ease as he scuffed a toe in the dirt of the cave. He avoided looking at the body of his fallen friend. He repeated, more than once, "It's Nate's fault. He brought a rope that is too short. Then he got hurt when he fell, because the rope was too short." Pausing for a moment from repeating this accusation, Blake asked, "Which one of you has a cell phone? We'll call for help."

"I…I don't HAVE a cell phone, "Josh replied. "My dad says they're too expensive. My sister had one. She texted $300 in one month. Now my dad says I can't have one."

"Kitra?"

Kitra's face was an ashy, chalky shade. She was breathing shallowly. She had never seen a bloody dead body up close. Someone she knew personally. Someone her own age. She brought a small pink cased phone from her backpack. Trying to dial her cell phone, she said, "It's no use. There's no reception down here." She threw the phone back in her backpack in frustration and added, "Why didn't YOU bring one, Blake? Why do you just blame us for everything that goes wrong?"

Shock was setting in. She joined Josh in softly sobbing. She was shivering. Kitra resumed muttering, "Poor Nate! Poor Nate!"

"I did bring one," Blake said. "But mine doesn't get any reception down here, either. I already tried it. So, we have to figure out how to get this old rope re-attached to what we can see of the nylon rope. We have to make it longer so we can get out! Ditch the 'poor Nate' routine. It's going to be poor *US*, unless we re-attach the usable remnant of the old rope to the nylon rope. I pounded that iron stake into the ground myself. That thing is secure. Don't blame me because Nate fell! He didn't get us a long-enough ladder. And Josh dropped mine. The first rope *was* long enough." Blake rubbed his long-sleeved plaid shirt sleeve across his nose.

"What do you think happened to Nate?" Kitra looked helplessly from Josh to Blake for an answer.

"I—I don't know, Kitra. Something shredded the first rope. Remember? We found little pieces of it in the tunnel?" Josh looked shaken as he reminded Kitra of their journey down the left-hand side of the cave's two tunnels. Josh was spooked.

"I remember. But what do you think did it? What do you think happened?" Kitra wiped her own sleeve across her eyes to dry her tears, leaving a smear of dust and sweat on her right cheek. She sniffled slightly.

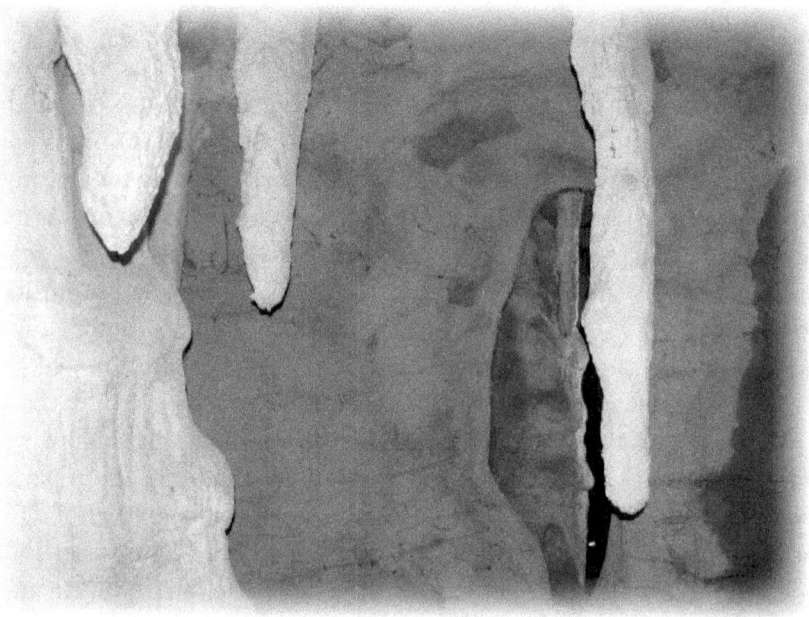

Blake said, "What's happened here is that our buddy Nate is a complete klutz. He fell off the rope ladder on his way down. Then he fell off the rope ladder on his way up." Blake spoke in a coarse matter-of-fact tone. "It really doesn't matter HOW he managed to fuck up this trip. What matters now is how we are going to get OUT of this hell-hole. Since you're the lightest, Kitra, we need to get a long enough segment of the hemp rope to tie to Josh's nylon rope. Josh and I will hold you up so you can reach it. If we use this part of my old rope—the one Josh dropped—(*here, Blake glared at Josh and held up the portion of the hemp rope that appeared usable*) we can shimmy up my rope to Nate's rope and out of the cave to safety. The climb will be just like the one we have to do in gym class every year."

Kitra looked at Blake. Her eyes were tear-filled turquoise pools. Josh said nothing. He tried to compose himself. He was thinking many things. He was thinking, *Would some creature want pieces of twine for a nest? How pissed off at me are my mom and dad going to be when I don't get home for dinner before dark. How dumb is it that we don't have at least ONE cell phone that works! I always flunk rope-climbing in gym class. Every time. Every year. Can I do what Blake is proposing? Can Kitra?*

But Josh said nothing.

I don't need to get pounded. I have to deal with this. We've got to get out of here. And fast.

Josh and Blake dragged flat rocks to the landing area. They built up a platform to stand on. Blake was six feet tall. Despite that, the rope ladder was at least four feet above them in the well-like descent. The rope *had* to be made longer. There'd be no one staying below to offer a leg up, as they had with Nate. (And look how THAT turned out!) Blake and Josh would have to hoist Kitra up as high as possible. Then, they'd have to hold her there, steady, for as long as it took for her to re-attach the undamaged portion of the coarse manila hemp rope to the three-play nylon rope—if she could do it at all.

"Do you know how to make any Boy Scout knots?" Josh asked Kitra. When Josh earned his Eagle Scout badge, tying knots was a specialty. In fact, Blake had actually authorized Josh to tie the knots around the tree, despite his anger at him for dropping his father's rope on Saturday.

"Yeah. Right. I was tops in my Boy Scout class," Kitra said, sarcastically. She was frightened. Fear caused her to respond with sarcasm.

"Don't get smart with us. You *have* to know how to tie a knot securely enough so that we don't fall like Nate did," Blake said. "Josh can show you, if you don't know how."

"I'm sorry, Blake. I'm just really upset. Do you think a fall killed Nate? Did his fall rip his throat open like that?" Her voice quavered as Kitra waved an arm in the direction of Nate's lifeless body. She couldn't bear to actually look at her dead friend. If she did, she'd break down in tears again.

"Well, what else?" Blake said. Impatient. Condescending. Unwilling to consider any other explanation.

"Josh and I saw some remnants of twine in the left tunnel. Pieces. Torn up. Shredded. Like a bird might tear up to make a nest."

"Right," said Blake. "A bird did this." He rolled his eyes. Blake moved on without further comment, "Do you want Josh to show you how to tie a knot that might save our lives, or are you just going to spout nonsense?"

As Josh and Kitra embarked on a crash course in knot-tying, a strange, faint shuffling noise came from the left tunnel. At first, only Blake heard it. Josh and Kitra were involved in the intricacies of Knot-Tying 101.

"No, no, Kitra. You have to go under this part first and then over that part."

Josh was doing his best to show Kitra how to tie the strongest knot possible in the fastest amount of time. *The overhand knot and the figure eight might be easiest*, he reasoned. *Too bad I don't have time to teach her the Blake's Hitch, but that's too complicated.* The very name of the knot was ironic.

"Wait! Did you guys hear that?" Blake asked the absorbed duo. He pointed towards the left tunnel.

"Hear what?"

"That noise….that sound…sort of a shuffling sound. Didn't you hear it?"

"No, Blake. We didn't hear it. If you're so interested, why don't you go investigate?" Kitra was not listening to Blake's comments. She had already tied three knots that fell apart immediately. Josh was trying to think of easier-to-tie knots that still would hold the 170-pound Blake Norton. Blake was large for their eighth grade class. He'd repeated seventh grade. Now he was repeating eighth grade.

Blake said, "Maybe I will."

He pulled a piece of beef jerky from his knapsack with a defiant flourish, and took off down the left tunnel. Blake's flashlight beam reflected crazily off the walls of the tunnel as he disappeared around the bend. The sound of his footsteps echoed back to the duo. But Josh and Kitra were absorbed in the lesson at hand.

Just as Kitra felt confident that she could quickly tie a figure eight knot securely enough to save their lives, Blake reappeared, chewing on the beef jerky. Nonchalant. Clueless.

"Nothing down there," he said, motioning behind him.

As the two crouched on the floor of the cave turned to watch Blake's return, they could see the Trogloraptor Marchingtoni spider above his head. Blake was oblivious, unaware of the tremendous, six-eyed eight-legged spider. Dubbed "the cave robber," the new species had been discovered hanging from the roofs of caves in the area one month ago by spelunkers in the forests north of Clampton. Scientists were still studying it.

The half-dollar sized spider was a brand new species. Its claws, which had three distinct bends, were raptorial. It was a fierce, specialized predator. The small spiders that scientists found attached to strands of silk that they brought to the surface, were being compared to a phenomenon like Bigfoot in the Los Angeles papers. This particular honey-brown spider was the actual *SIZE* of Bigfoot.

All the smaller spiders brought in from caves by California Academy of Sciences arachnologist Charles E. Griswold and his colleagues were vicious-looking, but normal in size. The Trogloraptor spiders were now in a lab at the University of California in Berkeley. They refused to eat a variety of prey offered them. Scientists were unsure what the spiders ate. What was the prey of the Trogloraptor Marchingtoni spider?

This one had to be the Grand Daddy of all Trogloraptors. It was at least ten feet across. It hung from the roof of the cave, attached by deadly-looking golden-brown claws. A sticky spittle-like liquid dripped from its pincers. Its wasp-like brown body extended back behind lobster-like tentacles. The six eyes of the creature were intent on tracking Blake Norton's progress.

It was truly the most horrifying sight that Kitra Moon or Josh Wells had ever seen. The sight of the gigantic spider, hanging from the cave ceiling, even surpassed the horror they felt upon discovery of Nate's dead body. Josh and Kitra were so frightened they couldn't even cry out.

Josh grabbed Kitra with one hand, the rope with the other, and, with superhuman strength, fueled by terror and adrenaline, Josh single-handedly hoisted Kitra towards the bottom of the nylon rope ladder in the well-like entrance to the cave. Hemp rope segment in hand, Kitra inhaled sharply.

Calm. Keep calm.

She did her best to clear her head. *Remember what Josh just taught me about knots.*

Josh, the shorter of the two boys, stood absolutely still. He watched the spider tracking Blake Norton, who was still unaware of its menacing presence above his head.

Josh was mesmerized by the gigantic arachnid. He couldn't have moved quickly if his life depended on it, which it did. Josh simply did his best to hold Kitra aloft. *Still. Stand still,* he thought to himself. The veins in his forearms stood out with the exertion of holding the one hundred pound girl aloft as she frantically tied the knots needed for their escape.

"What's the matter with you two? Didn't you hear me? There's nothing down there? Why didn't you wait for me before hoisting Kitra up to reattach the rope?"

That was the last question Jake Norton would ever ask.

Kitra was frantically tying the coarse hemp rope to the bottom of the nylon three-ply boat rope ladder. She was concentrating like never before. Her fingers were shaking. The slippery nylon rope and the coarse hemp rope were not easily joined. The knot had to be good. She—they—had only one chance. Josh was not strong enough to hold Kitra above his head longer than a few minutes. Blake might be able to, but not Josh.

The Trogloraptor had other more immediate plans for Blake Norton.

As the final knot lengthened the nylon rope ladder to a distance that would allow Josh and Kitra to clamber to safety, the gigantic prehensile spider reached down for Blake in slow motion. Two of its eight legs lifted Blake Norton into the air. Surprised, the beef jerky fell from Blake's lips. The class bully became a rag doll impaled on a spear. An expression of shock spread across Blake's features. He cried out, startled.

Then, Blake unleashed a blood-curdling scream. It was the full-throated beller of a man in intense pain. Someone taken completely unaware. A creature who recognizes extreme danger, but can do nothing to avert the inevitable. The sound of a soldier mortally wounded by shrapnel. The agonized howl of a brutalized victim. A death cry. There was a rending, tearing sound. The crunching, snapping noise represented the worst imaginable horror the human body can endure.

Now, the rope was tied. Kitra shimmied up the rope. She was acutely aware that Josh needed to quickly follow her.

Would Kitra be able to climb fast enough to make it to the upper portion of the rope with actual ladder-like steps? Would there be enough time for Josh to follow her? The Cave Robber spider was distracted by its current task: making a light snack out of Blake Norton.

Kitra reached the rope ladder, nearly home free. She cried out:

"Josh! Follow me! Now! Come on!"

There was no answer.

Kitra was out. She was above ground. She must get help. But who? Where? How?

She ran for the path back to the small convenience store where she had bought the beef jerky. It was not as far as the town itself. *Mr. Graham! Mr. Graham can help me*, she thought. Mr. Graham was a Vietnam War veteran. He owned and operated the small combination gas station/ convenience store where Kitra bought the beef jerky—which seemed like it had been weeks earlier.

As Kitra ran up the path towards the small convenience store, she was trembling. Her heart pounded in her chest like a frightened bird.

"Mr. Graham! Mr. Graham! Come quick!"

A slightly hunched figure with a full beard and gray-white hair emerged from the convenience store. George Graham, a helicopter pilot, was shot down twice in 'Nam. He broke his back. As a result, George couldn't move as fast as a terrified thirteen-year-old girl.

"What's the matter, Kitra? What's happened?"

Kitra quickly filled the grizzled war veteran in. "Come quick! It's Josh!"

The sixty-eight-year-old former helicopter pilot grabbed an axe embedded in a pile of logs he'd been splitting behind the store.

"Kitra. Wait! I have a lightweight ladder. We should take it. I'm not sure I trust your rope ladder, after what you've told me." Each grabbed an end of the lightweight aluminum ladder leaning against the back of the small store. It slowed them down slightly, but George felt it was necessary to assure safe access to and exit from the cave.

It took ten minutes to reach the cave entrance. The duo positioned the ladder. George Graham insisted on being the first to enter the cave.

When they reached the bottom of the ladder, there was no sign of Josh. Nate's body lay where it had been, undisturbed. Kitra still could not look in the direction of her dead friend. She was hyper-ventilating. She knew she'd be too upset to help Mr. Graham if she became any more upset.

Stay calm. Be calm. Chill, she told herself. Her teeth chattered with fear. She clenched her hands so tightly that her fingernails left marks in her palm.

A faint sound came from the right-hand tunnel, the tunnel Blake had explored. The tunnel where the Cave Robber lurked.

"This way!" Kitra shouted to George Graham. He hefted the heavy axe in his hand, unsure what he'd do with it if Kitra's tale of a gigantic spider were true. George Graham was brave. He'd volunteered for two tours in Nam. But George Graham despised spiders.

The two trotted quickly down the left tunnel, with Kitra and George taking turns shouting, "Josh! Josh! Where are you! Josh!"

There was no response. Kitra intuitively knew this was the correct direction.

A bend in the tunnel loomed.

As the duo rounded this corner, the cave opened into a larger room.

Along the perimeter of the room were gauzy cocoons, bound to the walls with white webbing. Within the cocoons—which varied in size from five to seven feet—living organisms were imprisoned. Some of the cocoon pods squirmed slightly with inner activity.

In the center of the room was a huge, gauzy, sticky web. Infrequently, a group of spiders will build webs together in the same area. One web found at Lake Tawakoni State Park in Texas in 2007, measured 200 yards (180 meters) across. A social cobweb. This social web was at least twice as large as the biggest one previously discovered in Texas. Immediately in the center of the web sat the Cave Robber spider. Silent. Waiting for victims. Huge. Hungry. Dangerous. The tremendous golden brown Cave Robber spider that had ripped Blake Norton apart like a child's toy rubbed two of its forelegs together, as though in anticipation of prey to come.

Smaller wolf spiders which actually run their prey down, came skittering towards the pair. Kitra quickly retreated to the highest point on a nearby promontory, while George swung the axe at the disgusting creatures. The Wolf Spiders retreated.

"George—we have to get close to the cocoons. We have to check them. Maybe Josh is in one of those things! Keep your eye on that monster spider in the center of the web. Warn me if it moves."

"Be careful," George said, fending off the last of the wolf pack spiders.

Kitra approached the cocoons, which were podlike in appearance. She immediately thought of the movie *Invasion of the Body Snatchers*. Or was it one of the *X-Files* movies where she'd been repulsed by a similar sight?

Within one of the cocoons, which was attached to a stalagmite, she could see her friend Josh's face. He was unconscious. Kitra ripped at the white, webbed, gauzy cobweb to reveal more of her friend. She succeeded in removing most of the cotton candy like substance from around Josh's body. When she pulled him completely from the center of the pod-like prison, Josh began to move slightly. Some of the other cocoon victims were animals—wolves, deer, dogs, cats. None but Josh was human. Only Josh remained alive.

"George! George! Help me carry Josh to the ladder. He's coming around."

Josh did appear to be regaining consciousness. He was awakening from the Limbo of the Cave Robber's prison.

"What happened? What is that thing?" Josh mumbled, regaining consciousness.

"Don't worry about that now, Josh. The main thing is to get you—to get us—out of here!"

The trio began their retreat to the cave exit, pursued by skittering wolf spiders. George repeatedly drove the cluster of spiders back with his axe. Kitra removed her jacket. She used the jacket to swat the arachnids away from her feet and ankles. A few of the tenacious insects crawled up her bare leg. George and Kitra were supporting Josh between them. Josh half-stumbled and was half-dragged towards George's ladder.

"What about that gigantic spider?" George asked Kitra. He shuddered slightly.

"We'll have to come back with flame-throwers. Or seal the cave entrance. But right now we have to get Josh medical help. He may have been bitten. I think Josh was being stored by the spider for food. We can't be too careful. Pray that that thing doesn't come after us." She kicked at the small, skittering Wolf Spiders, "These things are bad enough."

"I'll say!" agreed George, as he, once again, took a swipe at a black throng of the Wolf Spiders.

The trio reached the landing area. Kitra climbed up first. George would need to help guide Josh to safety, supporting him if necessary.

It took twenty minutes for the trio to reach the grassy area outside the mouth of the cave.

Kitra collapsed on the damp grass. Out of breath. Sobbing.

"That was the ugliest spider I ever saw in my life...and the biggest! What kind was it?" George Graham asked, incredulity evident in his tone of voice.

"I don't know, Mr. Graham. All I know is that it killed Blake. It probably killed Nate, too."

George slowly rose to his feet. His broken back ached. His pulse was pounding. He said, "Let's get Josh to a hospital. We'll come back later and destroy the nest below ground. Nobody—no living thing... should be kept in limbo, waiting for something like *that* to finish it off. That was worse than anything I saw in 'Nam." George removed his green John

Deere baseball cap and slapped it against his right thigh. He was trying mightily to regain his composure.

Scientists soon discovered what the Cave Robber Spider preyed upon. The Cave Robbers were carnivorous.

Norton's Cave was sealed, preventing the Cave Robber from ever killing again.

Circle Two: Lust

The Monster Within

John O'Connor hated Brian Frederickson with an all-consuming passion.

That son-of-a-bitch Frederickson STOLE my girlfriend. Flat-out stole her. One minute she's in MY bed. Next minute, she's screwing Frederickson. Not only do I have to work for the jerk, now I have to watch Jennifer come and go with him every damn day. Right outside my window! Right across the road!

O'Connor's blood pressure rose perilously just thinking about Jennifer's betrayal. It was May 30, 2013. He and Jennifer had been a couple since Christmas. The six happiest months of John O'Connor's life.

As much as John O'Connor hated Brian Frederickson, he was certain that Brian disliked *him* even more.

Good thing only the government at the Fort has the ability to hire and fire, thought John. *Fredrickson would LOVE to get rid of me!*

Sometimes, John wondered if Brian had purposely gone after Jennifer simply to spite him. Their years living across the road from one another had been a re-enactment of the Hatfields versus the McCoys. Constant disputes. Never-ending complaints. Quarrels over everything from where the garbage cans should (or should not) be placed to whether Brian drove too fast when he zoomed into his driveway at the end of the day.

Brian objected to John's dog, Scout. Brian claimed Scout was a "dangerous nuisance and a menace." Brian even reported the black Labrador to Sheriff Richardson. Brian complained about the noises he'd heard coming from John's basement, and blamed them on the beast. Brian accused John of shooting out the lone street light that usually illuminated their mutual gravel road. (*That light remained dark two months later.*).

All Brian's complaints originated BEFORE Brian Frederickson seduced Jennifer Reilly and invited her to move in with him. Brian paraded Jennifer around across the road from her former live-in boyfriend, right in front of John O'Connor's now-closed Venetian blinds—the bedroom blinds that did such a piss-poor job of shutting out the morning sun *AND* the lone street light. Once John shot out the street light with a bee bee gun, that situation improved. No light. No problem.

But Brian Frederickson *WAS* a problem for John O'Connor.

John thought Brian was an arrogant prick. He had often expressed this opinion to Jennifer when the two were together. *Of all the people at the fort,* John thought for the millionth time: *Brian Frederickson! I HATE that guy! It's not bad enough Jennifer dumps me. But for my boss? Brian's also the meanest member of our team.*

John did have to admit that Brian was smart. Brian got results. However, Brian got results by verbally abusing his employees. Many of the women employees broke down in tears. John thought, again, *I HATE that guy! I'll get even with him. Who does he think he is? Brian Frederickson stole my girl.*

John peered through the slats of his bedroom Venetian blinds. He wondered if the new couple knew he was watching them. John's mind raced. From here, he could see directly into Brian's family room. Jennifer sat on Brian's couch, waiting for her new love to return from work, much like Scout sat at John's back door, always eager to welcome him home. John's heart hurt. His hands clenched in helpless rage.

Outside, Brian emerged from his silver Hyundai Veracruz. Soon Brian and Jennifer would sit together on the couch. Her blonde head would rest on his shoulder. Divinely happy.

Probably watch the DVD of "Love, Actually" I gave her for Valentine's Day, John thought grimly.

John heated his TV dinner. Alone. Miserable. Obsessed. The unhappiest man in El Reno, Oklahoma. But John had a plan. It was one reason he was glad that the county had not bothered to fix the streetlight.

O'Connor glared out the window at Frederickson's impressive white frame home. The gravel on the road between them sparkled in the dying dusky light of Reno Road. The road was a remote rural byway outside Oklahoma City, close to Fort El Reno. In the twilight, the road looked as though it was paved with tiny diamonds.

John O'Connor was involved in cloning research at Fort El Reno. Dr. Frederickson, head of the entire department, was his boss. Jennifer conducted tours of the historic fort. She was a minimum wage employee with no particular skill set other than being drop-dead gorgeous. No security clearance. Majored in Communications. Thought she was going to be the

next Katie Couric. Now reduced to working as a glorified tour guide of isolated Fort El Reno, Oklahoma.

On a good day, Jennifer might show twenty people around the Fort. The only time large crowds showed up at Fort El Reno was for monthly ghost tours of the historic edifice, located at the junction of the Chisholm Trail and the Wells Fargo stagecoach crossing just off I40. A remount station, back when horses ruled.

Jennifer worked the ghost tours, too, escorting one group of twenty from among the one hundred or so tourists that showed up for the nighttime tours at Fort El Reno. Sometimes, the organizers required her to dress up and pretend to be a ghostly presence. She read her script like a trained parrot. Jennifer didn't make much money for her sporadic efforts. That was one reason she'd moved in with John O'Connor back in December.

Since Jennifer was a minimum wage employee, even John speculated that she might have jumped ship because Brian Frederickson got paid more than he did. Brian had more prestige. More power. And John remembered from his Social Psychology class that "power is the ability to manipulate others through a desired series of outcomes."

Why else would Jennifer leave me? We were happy together. Everything was perfect—until Brian Frederickson.

John's eyes, peering through the slats of the Venetian blinds, were dark, glowing coals, mirroring his inner turmoil.

John thought he and Jennifer were the perfect couple—until Jennifer sent him an e-mail: "I can't go out with you any more, John. You're too negative." Then, she moved out. From that moment on, Jennifer simply ignored him. She soon began dating the handsome new genius at the fort, Brian Frederickson.

It wasn't over a day after Jennifer's departure that the "For Sale" sign went up on the new couple's lawn. John noticed Jennifer's salsa red Prius parked in Brian's driveway. He couldn't believe his eyes.

Shortly after that, John began work on a secret experiment. Sequestered in his basement, John was constructing a clone. A look-alike. A being that would be completely under his control. The monster would resemble John O'Connor in every way. The John-twin would be a computer-driven robot indistinguishable from a human—a creation that John could program to do whatever he wanted it to do. John had seen a prototype on a television show starring Halle Berry , "Extant." *That humanoid was a little kid named Ethan*, he remembered. *Mine will look just like me*, he thought. *I'll call him Sean.*

When John conceived the idea, he mused, *I could rob a bank. I could send my clone to visit my senile Grandma in the nursing home. My clone could kill someone. Me? I'd be safe. A group of witnesses would swear I was far away when the murder occurred. With the advanced capabilities of the creature AND its built-in self-destruct feature, there'd be no danger. If anything went wrong, I could hit the self-destruct switch. They'd have to catch it, first, anyway. And I could program it to leave no trace of its maker.*

Like Dr. Frankenstein, John perfected his creature in secrecy. He began the project right after Jennifer left him for his asshole neighbor. Now, the monster was almost ready to be unleashed.

Most people thought the official research going on behind closed doors at Fort El Reno was harmless. Jennifer always pointed out the Fort El Reno Research Center during her tour, telling the few visitors in her group, "Researchers in our research center are at work helping develop strains of rice to reclaim lands ravaged by the tsunami in Thailand. They design many other projects to help mankind. Scientists are attempting to cure cancer with vaccines and working to stop the proliferation of disease."

Jennifer liked saying "proliferation." It was written in her script. She thought it made her sound smart. She recited whatever was written on the page and believed every word.

But most of Jennifer's script was a lie.

Government employees like John and Brian—highly trained scientists with degrees combining every high-tech discipline—were cloning animals. The doctors at work behind the dark doors of the restricted access building were developing hazardous viruses and bio-medical weaponry. They were conducting any number of illegal bio-medical experiments.

Typical government obfuscation, thought John O'Connor, back when he and Jennifer lived together and she would practice her G-rated spiel. *Create a cover story and stick with it.*

John was not allowed to tell Jennifer the truth about Fort El Reno's real purpose.

Brian Frederickson was forced to retain all members of his research team when Dr. Shelton left after suffering a major stroke.

Even that stupid cow Molly Clark, Brian thought. *The one who's always crying at the drop of a hat. She must have been voted "least likely to succeed" in high school. If only I could fire her! And, of course, I'd like to get rid of that obnoxious O'Connor, my neighbor.*

Just thinking of O'Connor's smug face and his damn dog made Brian Richardson frown.

It was while watching John and Jennifer in the cafeteria that the plan came to Brian. Brian was new. He had no idea that Jennifer was John's sweetheart. Jennifer was the only attractive woman on the entire base: a luscious blonde who could challenge Marilyn Monroe or Scarlett Johansson. She was gorgeous. John was the least attractive guy on Brian's team. Possibly the least attractive male on the planet. Short. Balding. Nose hair. Slightly pudgy. Poorly dressed.

What does Jennifer Reilly see in him? Brian thought, when he learned from their co-workers that they were a couple.

When Brian found out that Jennifer actually *lived* with the creepy neighbor in the crappy house across the gravel road from him, just off Interstate 40, near West Oklahoma City's Reno Road—the neighbor he hated—Brian formulated a plan.

Brian disliked everything about John. He hated his looks. He disliked John's annoying habit of asking so many questions at staff meetings that they all were forced to stay late. He despised John's mangy dog. And he was certain that Brian was responsible for shooting out the darkened street light.

Brian's next question: *I wonder what Jennifer Reilly would see in ME?*

Brian was good looking. Tall, dark and handsome in a way that drove women wild. Brian had never had any trouble attracting eligible females. Soon, he had no trouble seducing Jennifer Reilly.

Never a forgiving sort, Brian Frederickson set out to (a) steal John O'Connor's girlfriend and (b) get rid of John O'Connor from their mutual neighborhood. Brian would have liked to have been powerful enough to add (c): Fire John O'Connor. Brian's authority did not allow him to terminate employees without the approval of the higher-ups. Failing to achieve Point "B," Brian made plans with the local Century 21 realtor to put his house on the market and to move into town. But houses in the Oklahoma boonies

weren't exactly a red-hot commodity for folks purchasing homes. Both of them were stuck with John's peeking and peering until they sold their house. And both Jennifer and Brian endured John's hostile glares at work.

"Your ex-boyfriend is just plain creepy," he told Jennifer as she emerged from the shower, towel wrapped around her curvaceous form. "We'll get another place, far away from that Peeping Tom."

'But, Honey," Jennifer protested. "I told you. I only moved in with him because I couldn't afford the rent on my own. I never loved him."

Jennifer rested her damp blonde head on the handsome Brian's shoulder. She thanked her lucky stars that Brian had been transferred here from Baltimore after Dr. Shelton's stroke.

"Can't you do something about John, Honey? He keeps saying awful things about me on Facebook. He won't stop. I wish I'd never met that guy." Her large blue eyes fixed Brian with an imploring look.

Brian patted her reassuringly on the shoulder. He handed her a cup of coffee. (*Secretly, he hoped she'd drop the towel while reaching for the coffee cup.*) "I'll think of something, Honey. Don't worry. I'll make him stop."

Brian Frederickson had a plan. It tied in with his work. Yes, it would be a challenge. However, if a robot could be built capable of vacuuming and parking a car, one could be built that would take care of creepy John O'Connor. A robot didn't have to be built from metal. Brian Frederickson— graduate of Johns Hopkins—had bio-medical engineering knowledge and a medical background. He could clone a programmable creature. *After all, that Ethan humanoid creature is pretty convincing on "Extant,"* he thought.

Brian knew exactly what he wanted his clone to do.

Brian would uproot his new love interest. He would move both of them away from John O'Connor and his prying eyes. His clone could and would do all the things that Brian would never have the cojones to do. Shoot someone. Cut up a body. Bury a dog.

Who knew what Brian's creation would be capable of? *The sky's the limit,* Brian thought. He smiled slyly.

It was 6:00 p.m. on August 30th, 2014. The day had suddenly turned a sickly sepia-tinged brown, like an antique photograph. It made Brian think of the lighting in the film *The Godfather*. At 6 p.m. an E5 tornado 2.6 miles in diameter with softball-sized hail, traveled across the El Reno and Reno Road area at 300 mph, destroying everything in its path. Stripping the bark from trees.

The newly-replaced street light came on at 6: 43 p.m. on August 31, 2014. It illuminated five dead bodies: two heaps resembling clothing store dummies. Two male victims. One female victim, with long blonde hair. One black Labrador Retriever. Just as John O'Connor was releasing his creation upon Brian Frederickson, Brian Frederickson responded in kind.

Then nature turned up the dial. A storm that sounded like a freight train bore down upon the rural area, where the secluded homes of Brian and John were located, on Reno Road. Everything in the tornado's path was destroyed. At 6:42 p.m. CDT, the storm five miles east of Yukon moved down I40, towards Bethany and Richland. The storm was extremely dangerous. A life-threatening tornado—possibly the worst in history. It wiped out entire developments. Killed anything in its path. Played hell with the feud over a beautiful blonde.

Although both houses were totally destroyed, the newly replaced street light stood untouched, a beacon of light. When it came on outside the ruins of John O'Connor's ranch house on August 31st, 2014, it revealed death and destruction beyond anything the lust-filled rivals for Jennifer Reilly's affections could have imagined.

The newly-replaced street light—sole survivor of the sordid scheming of two neighbors who became arch-enemies (*and* of an E5 tornado)—shone brightly on total devastation that rivaled Hiroshima. And the streetlight illuminated another reality.

Sometimes, when people shine a light on their monsters, they find out how similar their monsters really are.

Circle Three: Gluttony

The Battle of Gate Pa

April 29, 1864

Rawiri Puhirake circulated amongst his Nai Te Rangi New Zealand warriors.

"Do not talk. Do not speak. Do not whisper. Be as silent as the ghosts of your ancestors."

The men were crouched in a rabbit warren of tunnels dug beneath the surface of the New Zealand hill known as Gate Pa. They had worked on the site for days, making it nearly invisible to the British, three hundred of whom would come against them at daybreak. Rawiri knew they would come. He had guaranteed it. He invited the British to do battle at a certain time, in that certain place, with a carefully worded message. The challenge was phrased in excellent English. It was transcribed onto parchment using elegant calligraphy.

The message, headed *Potiriwhi District of Tauranga, March 28, 1864*, read:

> *To the Colonel:*
> Friend, salutations to you. The end of that, friend, do you give heed to our laws for (regulating) the fight.
> Rule 1: If wounded or captured whole and butt of the musket.
> Rule 2: If any Pakeha being a soldier by name shall be traveling unarmed and meet me, he will be captured and handed over to the direction of the law.
> Rule 3: The soldier who flees, being carried away by his fears, and goes to the house of the priest with his gun, even though carrying arms, will be saved; I will not go there.

Rule 4: The unarmed Pakehas, women and children will be spared.

The end.

These are binding laws for Tauranga.

By:

Terea Puimanuka

Wi Kotiro

Pine Anopu

Kereti

Pateriki

Rawiri Puhiraki

Rawiri—who had been well-educated by A.N. Brown and his wife Christina (*and, before Christina, by Brown's first wife, Charlotte*), missionaries at The Elms—was an outstanding student. He easily mastered English. He wrote in a beautiful cursive handwriting, inviting commanding Brigadier General Carey to fight at Gate Pa.

The letter was so succinct in its composition, so grandly executed in a formal, stilted style, laying out the exact time of day and location of the battle, that it was tantamount to baiting the Brigadier General. Brigadier General Carey had, so far, refused to engage in battle with the Maori, other than defensively.

It was merely adhering to the Rules of War in that day, time and place. Courtly. Chivalrous. Polite. The Rules of Engagement had been hammered out in discussion with the signers of the invitation, the authors of the pact. When, seven weeks later, the brilliant Rawiri was killed in a different battle, the rules of engagement would be found sewn into the lining of the coat of Ngai TeRangi (*one of the chief authors of the document*) along with these words: "If thine enemy hungers, feed him; if he thirsts, give him drink."

The invitation to take up arms was successful. It succeeded in convincing the British to move militarily against the native peoples of New Zealand in the Tauranga Campaign. After the courtly invitation to do battle at Gate Pa, the General was determined to fight to put down the opposition he termed "savages" and "niggers."

Missionary A.N. Brown, who had been at The Elms from 1830 (*and remained at The Elms until 1887*), had mixed emotions. He was British, but he and his two wives had come to know the natives well. They had come to appreciate the Maori. At this point, Missionary Brown had known the Maori for thirty-four years. He had taught many of them to read and write English. The Maori were good students. They learned quickly and were quite clever.

A church—a prominent feature of The Elms—was established to convert the Maori to Christianity. Therefore, it was with very mixed emotions that Brown and his second wife, Christina (*first wife Charlotte had died in 1859*), hosted a grand dinner for the British officers on the eve of the battle.

April 28, 1864, The Elms, Gate Pa, New Zealand, Evening

Rather than apprehension about tomorrow's battle, the men appeared to be in a festive mood. They feasted in a gluttonous fashion. Suckling pig. Local produce. All manner of beverages. Good Scotch whiskey. Christina favored the assembled ten officers with songs on the piano following the meal.

"Aren't you fearful that you or some of your men will fall tomorrow?" Christina asked Brigadier General Carey as they dined. She shivered slightly as she addressed this sensitive question to the General, seated to her right. He wiped his mouth with the white linen napkin before responding. His fingers were greasy from tearing the legs from a small, cooked, quail.

"Pshaw, my good woman. They are a half-naked, poorly armed bunch of savages, outnumbered ten to one by well-trained British troops. We have 1,650 men available to us. Only three hundred will march tomorrow. I doubt if we need *that* many. We shall bombard them with four batteries of artillery from a range of 350 to 800 meters for eight hours before we advance upon the poor devils."

The General sipped from his cup. He fixed Christina with a look of utter confidence. Then he continued, "By then, if they haven't run off, they will wish they had." Carey smiled a wry smile. The nine officers listening at the table chuckled politely in agreement. "In fact, I shall send troops behind the battlefield, to make sure the savages don't try to sneak away into the morning mist and flee to the hills." General Carey took another drink from his tumbler of good British ale. His actions conveyed to Christina that the subject was closed.

The dining room for the feast the night before the battle was no more than twelve feet by ten feet. Narrow. A shoebox shape. With the table, the breakfront, the piano and the hutch usually containing Charlotte's prized china (*displayed there when it wasn't in use*), there was barely room to move around the outside of the burnished wooden table.

Directly to the left of the dining room was Reverend Brown's office. Very tiny. Beautiful wood everywhere. Barely enough room for his desk. Trophies on the wall, along with guns.

The British soldiers were in fine spirits at dinner that night, gluttonously relishing the opportunity to consume a fine home-cooked Elms meal. Unconcerned. Almost nonchalant.

"Tomorrow, we will put down the savages, once and for all," Brigadier General Cary said with confidence. The 1,650 men the British had at their disposal were distributed this way—700 from the 68th Regiment, 420 from the Naval Bay, 300 from the 43rd Regiment, 50 from the Royal Artillery and 180 from, variously, the 12th, 14th, 40th, and 65th regiments. The natives were badly outnumbered. The British had vastly superior weapons.

Addressing the subject of the battle that was to come on the morning following this sumptuous feast, Brigadier General George Cary said, "We will move on them at daybreak. We have four batteries of artillery. In addition to the 110 pound Armstrong gun, we have two forty pounders and two six pound Armstrong guns. In addition, we have two 24-pound howitzers. Two eight inch mortars. Six Coehorn mortars. What do the savages have? Knives? Rocks?"

The British officers laughed openly at the last dismissive remark. The mood on the eve of battle rivaled that of the Mexican troops under Santa Ana at the Alamo. The Mexican troops had reveled the night before their assault on the fort with mariachi music, the festive strains drifting back to the defenders of the San Antonio Fort. The British officers this night did not have an accurate impression of the enemy they would face on the morrow, nor did they give the Maori the respect that they deserved.

Rawiri Puhuraki, the great Maori strategist, continued to rally his troops throughout the night. He moved amongst them stealthily as they crouched in their trenches, waiting patiently. Rawiri urged complete silence.

"Do not let them know where we are. Do not let them know how many we are. Keep perfect silence until I give the signal to fire. Now, who will go with me to take the white picket fence that surrounds the garden at The Elms?" asked Rawiri.

Rawiri smiled as two eager young volunteers jumped up to join him.

The three Maori approached under cover of darkness. They quietly dug up the white picket fence that surrounded a vegetable patch. The tinny piano playing of Christina Brown wafted from the open window while the natives worked silently under the full moon, and the officers inside gorged themselves while listening to the playing of their hostess.

The Maori carried the fence back to the ramparts of their home-made trenches, aligning the sharpened planks so that any advancing soldier would have a sharp, pointed stake aimed at his mid-section to navigate before he could move on to breach the Maori trenches. As the Maori re-buried the fence, they smiled with pleasure at the irony of their action. They were using a picket fence from British property as a weapon against those very British. Rawiri was amused. He was filled with great good humor at the justice of turning a picket fence belonging to the enemy into a weapon to be used *against* the enemy, all while tomorrow's combatants supped within The Elms, singing songs, eating, and sipping tea.

The officers within The Elms with the Browns continued to enjoy the wild boar, suckling pig, wild turkey, quail, British wines and whiskeys imported from London, and other delicacies of the house. The ten officers left the table quite full of themselves in both body and soul.

The next day, only one of the officers sitting at The Elms table on April 28th would still be alive. The medical officer was the sole surviver.

April 29, 1864, Dawn, Gate Pa, New Zealand

The British began the battle at dawn by shelling thirty tons of metal at the enemy for a full eight hours. The Maori, however, for the first time in recorded wartime history, creatively had improvised trenches. This technique would later be used extensively in World Wars I and II. The heavy artillery shells sailed harmlessly over the trenches where the Maori silently crouched, awaiting the advance of their opposition. The Maori prepared for the moment when the enemy soldiers would enter the Killing Zone.

Although fifteen Maori died, the battle was pronounced a rout for the British. It was considered a disaster by British standards. Local newspapers reported that the British forces were "trampled in the dust by a horde of half-naked, half-armed savages." One paper described the Maori battle plan as "a remarkable tactical ploy, brilliantly implemented as well as brilliantly conceived."

The British did not anticipate that their artillery would sail harmlessly over the heads of their opponents. Soon, the unsuspecting Brits were engaged in hand-to-hand warfare with courageous Maori warriors decorated with the striking tattoos of their tribe. The re-purposing of the white picket fence from The Elms proved to be just one of many hurdles that caused the troops to become paralyzed with fear. If they could find a way out, they streamed from the Killing Zone in frantic retreat.

All the other officers, wounded, dying or already dead, would be brought back to the small house at The Elms, a building roughly large enough for ten people to inhabit at once. Eighty wounded men were cared for in the house. Most of the soldiers would be placed on the grassy lawn outside. Thirty-one of the British soldiers would die, nine of them the very same officers who had dined in such splendor the night before the battle. Among them was an officer named Hamilton.

After the British infantry marched into the maze of pits covered over with raupo shares (a New Zealand bulrush, *Typha orientalis*, with sword-shaped leaves, traditionally used for construction and decoration), they began to die. They marched two deep. Sailors on the right. Side-by-side under the breast of the hill until they were seventy yards from the Maori trenches. There they halted.

Hamilton exhorted the men, "Steady now, men. This will all be over soon." Hamilton was right. But his prediction of an easy British victory was incorrect. Like the other soldiers, he was oblivious to the true nature of the enemy.

A member of the First company, Glover Garland, described Maori warriors, decorated with war paint and provoking fear by their very appearance, poking their rifles out of the trenches when only three yards away. They killed many of the British soldiers, inflicting fatal head wounds. Captain Hay from the ship the *Harrier* was critically wounded. Bob Glover found his younger brother suffering from a major injury to his head, a nearly crushing blow above his left ear. Bob began shouting over the din, his voice reflecting shock and fear, "Will no one help my brother?"

Utterton of the Second company and Hamilton and Clark of the Third company and Moran and young Glover of the Fourth company: all lay dead. Hamilton—who had reassured the men just moments before—was on his back, a gory corpse. When young Glover was lifted up amidst all the confusion, his brains were clearly visible spilling from his gaping head wound.

"It was so hot," Bob Glover said later. "So hot. The men were paralyzed with fear. They didn't expect anything like this. They didn't know whether to retreat or to press forward." Sergeant Major Vance lay face-down in front of them, dead and grotesquely disfigured. Corporal Booth could be heard moaning, "Don't leave me! Don't leave me!" His comrades in arms were trying to find a way out of the maze. Amidst the heat and panic and sound of gunshot, all was chaos. Confusion.

Hamilton, one of The Elms officer dinner guests, had tried valiantly to rally the bewildered, panic-stricken men. He seized a rifle. Held it aloft. Shouted, "Come on, Men! Follow me!" As Hamilton uttered the last sentence, he was fatally shot, collapsing as quietly as he had hitherto been loudly exhorting his troops.

It was a terrible defeat for the British, but a wonderful victory for Rawiri Puhurike and his Maori natives. What made the victory even more gratifying was the code the natives had agreed upon before the battle. The human rules of engagement that the so-called "savages" imposed on themselves and on the British did not go unremarked. The Maoris' gallant behavior under the leadership of the forty-year-old Rawiri later influenced the colonial governor to permit the Maori to keep their lands and live peacefully amongst the British.

Thirty-one of the British were killed. Eighty were wounded, including nine of the ten officers who dined the night before the battle with the Browns. Only fifteen Maori were killed. The Battle of Gate Pa became known as "the single most devastating British defeat in the New Zealand Wars." Later, word spread that some of the Brits were cut down by friendly fire as they circled behind the trench area, as ordered by their commanding officers.

The great Maori chiefs, (Ngai Te Rangi, Te Reweti, Eru Puhirake, Tikitu, Te Kani, Te Rangihav, Te Wharepouri and the master tactician,

Rawiri Puhirake) agreed, seven weeks later when the British returned to New Zealand's Bay of Plenty and resumed the Tauranga Campaign, to cease fighting. At that battle seven weeks later, Rawiri was killed. The chief architect of the Rules of Engagement also died in the fighting. The turnaround from the May battle convinced the Maori to agree to terms in order to stop the slaughter.

Make no mistake: the Maori won and revolutionized warfare forever.

The bellicose Brigadier General George Carey agreed, after the Battle of Gate Pa, that defensive action, only, might be the better, wiser course of action. He had not expected to face an opponent so fierce, smart and fearless.

Not only had the Battle of Gate Pa introduced the world to trench warfare for the first time (*just as the Battle of Ypres in World War I was the first use of chemical warfare*), but the primarily peaceful Maori agreed to lay down their weapons "if we can have full claims over our lands and the Governor will promise to see that no harm befalls us."

Unlike the American Indians of the western United States, promises made to the Maori were kept. The fighting ended with peace in New Zealand, a new-found respect for the native inhabitants, and an entirely new way of warfare that would endure forever.

Circle Four: Avarice & Prodigality

Boxed In

Summer, 1986:

"All my drug contacts are gone. I can't deal cocaine any more. When the cops busted me, I had ten grand in my hand! To stay out of jail, I had to rat out my suppliers, Babe. No more four grand a week. You're going to have to go back to work. I don't know what-the-hell I'm going to do to get my hands on that kind of money again!"

Danny Edmunds ran his hands through his curly black hair.

"Damn! That was great cash. It reminded me of life on the river with my folks in the big house—before they kicked me out."

Danny took another swig of his beer at the Kiki Lounge, where he was talking with live-in girlfriend, Nancy Rush.

"But, Danny! You said I could take the summer off." Nancy looked crestfallen.

"I know, Babe. That was before the cops busted me. My only hope of staying out of jail was to give up my suppliers. I had to quit dealing. Cold turkey. Which I did. My attorney says cooperating will keep me out of the slammer. But I am now officially unemployed and looking for a new source of income."

He smiled a fetching smile. Nancy didn't return it. "Aw…come on, Babe. Can't I be a kept man for a while?" Danny smiled again and reached for her hand across the bar where Nancy was bartending. She pulled back from his impromptu embrace.

Nancy tried to appear pleased. She didn't feel the emotion.

41

She planned on quitting this place next week. It was one of three menial jobs she worked. Now she was being told that late nights after long days would not end any time soon.

So much for "taking the summer off," she thought.

"Why can't you use your electrician's card, Danny? Electricians make good money!" This idea had just occurred to Nancy.

Danny fixed her with a stare that said, "How stupid can you be" (*at least he hadn't said it aloud—this time*). He asked, "Do you know any electricians who make $4 grand a week? I sure don't. 'Cause that's how much I was raking in before I got busted."

"You could go straight, Danny. You could work; I could work. Make a home for Ben—for the three of us. We could be a real family."

"Babe—you already work three jobs. What do you make a year? Twenty thousand, maybe? We were making $16 grand *a month*. Do you know how much that is a year? $832,000—that's how much. Nope. I gotta' put on my thinking cap. I have to figure out a way to score some major dough. Fast."

Nancy was upset. She didn't like working this hard, true. But she didn't want to always be looking over her shoulder wondering when the police would show up.

What kind of an example are Danny and I setting for Ben? she thought. Ben was only ten years old. He idolized Danny.

Still, Danny is good to Ben, Nancy thought. *That is something.*

They lived in a nice townhouse in Bourbonnais. Danny took the young boy fishing and water skiing behind the small motorboat he had bought with the easy drug money, now gone.

Danny had introduced Nancy to the joys of free-basing cocaine. It was a lifestyle she had never experienced before. The sex was great. He treated her son well. He had been an excellent provider. Until now.

Nancy—an old-fashioned girl at heart—did not take up with Danny until he showed up with a suitcase at the Kiki Lounge, announcing that his wife kicked him out.

"Our marriage is over for good," Danny announced. Soon after, their divorce was finalized.

Nancy considered herself a good person, but she did have weaknesses. Drugs and sex. Those were her two biggest temptations. Danny represented both.

Danny came from a well-to-do family in Riverview, a tony neighborhood nestled along the Kankakee River in Kankakee, Illinois. His prodigal son ways caused a rift with his wealthy parents early in his life. When he was caught breaking into the neighbors' house, his parents banished him from home at the age of eighteen.

He went from living the good life in Riverview to participating in any scam or hustle that would mean easy money. Danny had a thing for fast cars, fast women and quick cash.

So it was that Danny Edmunds met Nancy Rush in a bar called the Teeyaahkiki. The name came from the Potawatomi word for "open country, exposed land." That word gave the entire city of Kankakee its name. The bar's patrons shortened the name to "the Kiki Lounge."

The bar was not in the chi chi Riverview area. It was in a less desirable part of town, Aroma Park. Nancy was a curvaceous blonde that day in 1986 when Danny first wandered in to have a beer. Just the way Danny liked his women. And Danny was cute: bedroom eyes, lean, tall, and sporting a mass of black, curly hair.

Though he was married at the time, he sidled over to the pretty girl with the peroxide blonde hair sitting at the bar with two girlfriends. He asked her if he could buy her a drink.

"No, thanks. I'm with my girlfriends. Plus, I see that you're married."

Nancy waved her beer bottle at Danny's left hand, indicating his wedding ring.

Danny smiled a charming smile. He was a handsome devil, but a devil nonetheless.

"I'm just barely married. She's about to kick me out."

"What for?"

He smiled. "Fooling around with other women."

"See?" said Nancy, with a smile. "I'm doing you a favor. Save your money. Take it home to your wife. Call me when you're *NOT* married."

She rose from the bar stool, turned to her girlfriends, who were nervously watching the verbal sparring match and said, "Let's go sit over there. In the booth. It looks more comfortable. Fewer distractions." She smiled back at him over her shoulder as she sashayed towards the dark horseshoe-shaped brown leather booth in the back.

Danny was not easily discouraged.

"Where do you live?" he asked the beautiful blonde.

"Not far from here," she answered.

Truth be told, Danny Edmunds *was* a good-looking guy. Nancy had no other beaus in her life at the moment. She was between men.

"You let me know when you're free and clear of your wife; then I'll tell you where I live," Nancy repeated.

She smiled an alluring smile and walked away with her girlfriends.

The trip into the bar that night, a few weeks later, with his suitcase in hand was Danny's signal to Nancy that he was now truly available. As Nancy said later, to her friends, "He was a pretty fast talker."

She smiled and turned away from the would-be suitor at the bar the night they first met. Resumed talking to her girlfriends. Prepared to move to the nearby booth.

"But how will I find you, if I don't know your address or phone number?" Danny asked.

"I'm here most nights. I work here part-time. Late. Right about now I'm done for the night. I get off when Georgie there takes over." Nancy nodded her blonde head at the older man working the bar, a weary-looking, pudgy, balding middle-aged guy wearing a stained white apron and a bow tie.

With that, Nancy and her two companions got up and moved to the booth near the back of the smoky, seedy bar. They ignored the smitten Edmunds. Nancy occasionally glanced over at Danny sitting at the bar when she thought he wasn't looking. She peered over her Miller Lite bottle, focusing one eye on the lanky, lean, curly-haired six foot-three inch would-be Romeo.

Danny had a sexy doe-eyed look. He looked like he'd just crawled out of bed. His naturally curly hair made him look like a Roman emperor, (*Nancy told him this later, in bed*). He was cute. No doubt about it.

As for Nancy: terrific figure. A great rack. Long blonde hair. Great personality. Big blue eyes. Nancy Rush didn't have difficulty attracting men.

Danny Edmunds' sexy good looks had Nancy's girlfriends tittering, "He's so cute!" one said to the other as the three slid into the circular booth over the brown Naugahyde leather.

Danny Edmunds seemed different. He had the look of someone who was going places. And he was planning on getting there fast.

Nancy had just broken up with a mean son-of-a-bitch who gave her a black eye and then took after her 10-year-old son, Ben, with a strap. Nancy, pregnant at fifteen, gave birth to Ben at sixteen. Her parents tried to get her to give Ben up, but Nancy was, deep down, a good girl. She wasn't the kind of girl who would give up her firstborn child. She never had a drinking problem until her life turned to shit.

Although she lived with her no-good-nik boyfriend to help pay the bills, she drew the line at serving as his personal punching bag. When he hit Ben, that was it.

Nancy moved out and took a third job at the Kiki Lounge to make ends meet. It was a late job, after her waitressing stint at the Red Rooster café till 7:00 p.m. And then there was dog-grooming at Freddy Fritters' Dog Bakery and Grooming Salon on weekends. Thank heavens her parents helped her babysit!

Ben, her young son, was her top priority. At 26 years old, with a 10-year-old, she was still a beauty. She had enough bad life experiences that she *could* have appeared old beyond her years. When she moved out on her last boyfriend, her finances were stretched to the breaking point.

Since then, Nancy had been flirting with alcohol to forget her troubles. She could drink free at the bar, but with three minimum wage jobs, she didn't have the money to develop or support a hard drug habit.

But Danny did.

Danny developed a taste for free-basing cocaine and had the connections to acquire it. He had learned that, even in a small town of 25,000 people, there was always someone with money who was willing to pay to get high. And Danny was there for them. As their dealer.

Or, at least, he was for a while.

Because he had grown up in Riverview, Danny knew all the rich families in town. The richest of all—practically his neighbors in Riverview— were the Jordans, owners of a media empire called American Publications.

The youngest Jordan, Steven, was just about Nancy's age. He, too, had a taste for the finer things in life. That meant that he didn't come into the Kiki Lounge in the less-desirable Aroma Park area. But Nancy met Steven once, at a Main Street Festival party.

She was with her last boyfriend. That low-life—an older, divorced businessman with money—moved in some of the better circles when he wasn't trying to beat up a woman with a young son. Nancy met Steven then. They spoke, but Steven Jordan was a quiet, slim man. He was intense about his work. He was also able to attract any number of eligible females, had he wished to do so.

Steven drove a Ferrari convertible. In a small town, that was an automatic signal of wealth and status. It was an Alpha Dog marker in a town of *any* size.

His Republican family was rumored to be among the richest in the town, if not the state. They owned TV stations and newspapers all over

Illinois and the Midwest. Rumor had it that Steven's grandfather, (*the former governor*), bought up the newspapers and TV stations so he could control and release *his* version of events, much like Fox News and Rupert Murdoch do today.

Steven purchased a Frank Lloyd Wright designed house at South Harrison Avenue and Kankakee Street, a beautiful example of the first Prairie Houses the famous architect built. Steven Jordan was planning on rehabbing it as a bachelor pad. The place had fallen on hard times. It needed a new roof, among other things.

Obviously, a young, single guy with that much money could have any girl in town. But Steven, unlike Danny, was not as good-looking or as confident. What he had over Danny in money didn't give him the self-esteem that he needed to score with women. Steven was prematurely balding with a rapidly receding hairline. His slight build and a noticeable stammer made him insecure around women.

Therefore, Steven didn't date much. He had noticed the pretty blonde (Nancy) when he met her on the arm of his casual business acquaintance at the Summer Festival on Main Street. But that was it. There were no trips to the Kiki Lounge where Nancy worked. Their paths did not cross at the Red Rooster restaurant or Freddy Fritter's Doggy Bakery in Aroma Park, either.

Steven Jordan was out of Nancy Rush's league, plain and simple. But he had been very courtly. He had been nice to her, when they briefly met. He had a shy engaging smile. His face lit up with a pleasant expression when he was introduced to Nancy as the grandson of a famous Republican Illinois governor and the neighbor of another. Nancy was properly impressed. Tongue-tied might have been a better description.

She was a 26-year-old single mother with a child, struggling to get by; Steven Jordan was on the fast track in life, even if he *was* currently driving solo in his Ferrari convertible. That was the only time Nancy Rush laid eyes on Steven Jordan.

Until that night.

September 2, 1986:

For weeks, things had been rocky between Danny and Nancy. He was becoming increasingly verbally abusive. It started to get worse when he lost his drug-dealing money.

Danny had been sleeping on the couch most of the last two months, as their relationship death-spiraled, deteriorating into arguments about Danny's need to find a job. While Nancy got up every day and reported to three jobs, just as she had pre-Danny, he was out in the garage, tinkering around with a three foot by six foot box. He told Nancy it was to store pool chemicals at his brother's house in Florida.

Every day Danny tinkered in the garage, door wide open. When he wasn't in the garage, he was asking Nancy to run him down to the hardware store or to pick him up at various locations. They lived literally two blocks from the police station. Numerous cop cars drove by the open garage during the summer, while Danny tinkered on his pet project, and Nancy fumed that he was wasting time he could have spent looking for work.

Nancy had no interest in watching Danny hammer things. She was too busy working. Caring for Ben. She didn't pay much attention to Danny's pet project. It seemed to have nothing to do with earning a living.

Once, when she did question him about his activities in the garage, he fixed her with a steely gaze of his always half-open, sexy slitted eyes and said, with a great deal of sarcasm, "Why, I'm going to open a lemonade stand so we can be rich again."

That was the last time she asked.

The oddest thing Danny requested that she do was to pick him up at a location eight miles west of the Indiana border in the middle of the night—an area surrounded by woods and little else.

Danny could be a cocky bastard when Nancy got bucky with him and asked too many questions. She knew nothing about the details of his illegal drug dealing. He didn't like her sticking her nose into his business and always told her, "It's for your own good. What you don't know won't hurt you." Since Nancy knew Danny had been dealing drugs for eight months, before he was arrested, she thought his phone call from the woods in the middle of the night on September 2nd, 1986, was drug-related.

It was a hot Indian summer night, with insects making a racket in the surrounding deserted farmland. The cicadas would screech for ten seconds. Twenty seconds. Thirty seconds of it was like the crescendoing music of an Alfred Hitchcock soundtrack by Bernard Herrmann. The sound put you on edge. Mosquitoes bred freely in the water-filled ditches. Nancy wished she had brought some bug repellent as she slapped away the pesky insects inside her white Ford Taurus.

It would be just like Danny to hook up with some new suppliers and get his ass thrown in the slammer again, she thought, while driving to pick him up.

She carefully followed the directions to get to the remote, isolated site. She had to turn onto a gravel road that ran alongside infertile sandy soil. She drove five miles, deep into a forested area.

As she pulled up at the site, she saw Danny standing there waiting. Nancy really needed to pee. She had drunk a couple of beers at the Kiki Lounge before starting off to pick Danny up. Lately, the drugs were in short supply, so alcohol was the only stimulant she could afford to dull her sense of daily defeat. Now the two Miller Lites were coming back to haunt her. Her bladder cried out for release.

Danny approached the car. Nancy rolled the window down to speak with him. She noticed that Danny had a shovel in his hand.

"What's with the shovel?" she asked, hurrying to open the door to the car so she could exit and go to the bathroom.

"Don't get out," Danny said, shoving the door shut on her foot. "And don't ask so many questions. You don't want to know the answers."

"I *have* to get out. I have to pee. Bad! I drank two beers at the club before you called. Why are you asking me to drive to the middle of nowhere at midnight, anyway?"

"It isn't midnight—yet," was Danny's only response, as he walked to the back of the vehicle after grabbing Nancy's keys from the ignition. He opened the trunk of her white Ford and threw the shovel in.

Nancy had split from the car by then. She was looking for a convenient spot to, as her girlfriends used to term it, "pop a squat." She saw a low-lying ditch with shrubbery nearby. She headed for the spot, Kleenex from her purse clutched in her right hand, while Danny was stowing the shovel in the trunk of her car.

Danny approached her as she was pulling up her underpants and jeans. "Here. Hold this."

"This" was a handgun. Nancy didn't know a 45 from a bazooka. She had no idea why Danny was giving her a handgun in the middle of the woods at midnight.

"Why do you have this? Did you need it to protect yourself from your new drug suppliers?" Nancy did not like guns. This one felt heavy and deadly in her clammy hands. The cicadas' loud cries echoed and built to an almost frightening climax. *Ching! Ching! Ching!* Feelings of alarm were increasing just like the noise of the cicadas chirping in concert in the nearby woods.

Just then, out of nowhere, a wraith-like creature staggered towards the pair. The headlights from Nancy's car were the only illumination, other than the light from the full moon. The figure's movements reminded of an old movie: "Meet the Mummy." He was bent over. Slowly navigating. Moving as though in a daze. Balance unsteady.

When the slight figure paused in the beam from her car headlights, Nancy recognized the slender man. She had met him once before: Steven Jordan. His hands were handcuffed. He was covered in sand and dirt. There was a piece of gray electrical tape over his mouth. His eyes were wide with fright. He looked as though he had been struck over his left cheekbone. Blood was dripping from a contusion over his left eye.

Nancy took in the scene, uncomprehending at first. Slowly, the realization dawned. Danny Edmunds was not out here dealing drugs. He was doing something far more sinister.

"Danny! What did you do? I know that guy! That's Steven Jordan! I met him once at the Festival on Main!"

"Well, aren't you the society maven," Danny growled, using a mincing tone of voice. "He's only one of the richest guys in the state. I kidnapped him. Now, I'm going to make him one million dollars poorer and us one million dollars richer. Ransom money. He'll barely miss it. Now that you know, you're going to help me."

"Danny! This is serious," Nancy said, gesticulating with the loaded pistol. She barely realized she was still holding the heavy revolver in her right hand. "I don't want any part of kidnapping anybody."

"Well, it isn't a matter of what *YOU* want, Babe. He's here. And we're here. And the coffin is over there." (*Danny jerked his head towards the shallow ditch in the shadows.*) "At least, it'll *be* his coffin if his family doesn't come up with a million bucks toot suite." With that, he looked at the manacled victim and shouted, "What do you think you're doing? Get back over there!" Danny pointed toward the grave he had dug in the sandy soil. It had twenty-foot PVC pipes protruding from the lid, which Steven Jordan had somehow managed to dislodge. There was no soil fill on top of the box yet; Steven Jordan had not yet been boxed in for good.

"Danny, I won't have anything to do with kidnapping and murder. Let's just take him back. We'll let him off near his house."

"You really are a dumb bitch, aren't you?" Danny responded derisively to Nancy's suggestion.

That's when Nancy fired the gun. She said, later, that she had no intention of shooting anyone. That the gun merely misfired. The bullet hit Danny in the left leg, shattering his patella. He immediately fell to the ground, moaning in pain. Clutching his knee. Shouting things at Nancy that were ill-advised.

By then, Steven Jordan—bruised and battered, but still alive—had made his way to Nancy's side. She reached over with her left hand and ripped the gray electrical tape from his mouth.

"Thank you! Thank you!" he said, through bloody lips. "I asked him if he was sure that contraption of his was going to work. He told me I was going to be fine. It's rigged with a light hooked to an automobile battery. There's a one-gallon jug of water, some candy bars, some gum, a flashlight. There are PVC pipes for air. Who knows if *THAT* will work?"

Nancy screamed at Danny, still writhing in pain on the ground, "Is *THIS* what you've been working on in the garage? You told me it was to hold chemicals for your brother's pool in Florida." She was indignant.

Still whimpering with pain as he lay on the ground, bleeding, Danny looked up and snarled at the woman he once loved, "See? You're just proving once again that you ARE a dumb bitch!"

"Don't call me that!" Nancy exploded. It was all she could do to keep herself from firing the gun again.

Steven, meanwhile, began to give Nancy instructions. He was wearing handcuffs with a lengthy chain connecting the two cuffs. Steven said, "Shoot the chain. Aim in the middle. Then I can get my hands free."

"Are you sure it's safe?"

Steven Jordan, visibly shaken, managed a short laugh.

"Is ANY of this safe? He nearly buried me alive in that box. I managed to keep the lid from closing. Now, I'm out. I say we put *HIM* in the box. He says it's 'safe.' Let *him* check it out. We'll head to town. Notify the authorities."

Nancy was conflicted. She didn't want any part of a kidnapping scheme, but she wasn't sure that she wanted to place her injured boyfriend (*or anyone else*) in a plywood coffin and bury that individual alive, either.

"Don't worry," Steven said softly. "Your friend has assured me that it's perfectly safe. We'll notify the cops. They have to be looking for me. I'll vouch for you. Tell them you knew nothing about this. That you helped me. You just saved my life. We'll only know whether his device IS safe after we put Lover Boy into his own coffin contraption. Hold the gun on him while I drag him over to the box."

Nancy had already done as Steven asked, shooting the chain joining the handcuffs. The shots echoed in her ears, shattering the silence and challenging the volume of the ubiquitous cicadas. The recoil of the gun surprised her. She knew next-to-nothing about guns. Nancy stood quietly at the site, training the small handgun on Danny as Steven pulled him towards the grave. She was seething at Danny's multiple put-downs and insults. They had increased in frequency and vitriol ever since his drug bust, after the easy money dried up.

Danny was bigger than Steven, but he was in great pain from his shattered knee. Screaming with every inch he was dragged. The buried box was not far away. It took only seconds to tumble Danny's body into the three-by-six-foot coffin.

"Don't leave me here!" Danny screamed, as Steven placed the plywood lid atop the casket-like structure.

"Why not?" Steven responded. "You told me it was perfectly safe! If it was safe for ME, it should be safe for YOU. We'll send the cops back to get you."

The two unlikely allies got into Nancy's small white Taurus and headed for town.

Six Months Later:

The wedding was a small family affair, held in the revamped Frank Lloyd Wright house that had been instrumental in Steven Jordan's kidnapping. A telephone call made to Steven the night of September second by someone impersonating a police officer had informed Steven that there was a break-in at the Frank Lloyd Wright house. Steven was told to go to the site immediately.

Of course, the bogus break-in notification from the police imposter was just Danny Edmonds' way of getting Steven Jordan alone. As Jordan attempted to enter his detached garage, Danny waited in the shadows, gun in hand.

After making the much-smaller Steven get into the trunk, Danny forced him to record a ransom message demanding one million dollars. Unfortunately, the recording quality was so poor that Steven's father and brother could barely make out the message. The directions for delivering the money were also unintelligible. Just another of Danny Edmunds' schemes gone awry. *(Yet it was Danny calling Nancy "dumb!")*

By the time the police returned to the remote site near the Indiana border where Danny had attempted to bury his victim alive, Danny Edmonds was dead. The coroner's office said the construction of the coffin, including the twenty-foot pipe for oxygen, was faulty. The pipe did not allow enough air to support life for more than three or four hours. Edmunds had a bad heart. He either died from asphyxiation or a heart attack. Either way, it was a horrible way to go. It would have been Steven Jordan who died in a plywood box, if Nancy had not intervened.

Because of all the publicity surrounding the kidnapping, the Jordan family wanted to avoid attracting any additional attention. Therefore, the wedding of their youngest son and heir was a very hush-hush affair.

After the ceremony, the shy millionaire and his blonde bride flew off to the Bahamas on a private honeymoon. As they drove away from the Frank Lloyd Wright house, a ten-year-old boy who had just attached "Just Married" signs to the gleaming Ferrari smiled happily. He waved good-bye to the newlyweds as they disappeared in the distance.

Circle Five:
Wrath & Sullenness

Do Not Go Gently

Inever thought about dying. It never occurred to me that I'd *ever* die.
Oh, sure, death comes for the Archbishop, and all that literary rot, but
it wouldn't come for me for a long, long time. If ever.

Probably part of the reason I thought I was immortal was that for a
long time, in childhood, I bought into the religious mythology surrounding
death. I was raised Catholic. That says it all. Heaven. Hell. Purgatory.
Limbo. (*Except then they got rid of limbo—or was that Purgatory?*) The
Baltimore Catechism.

Regardless of which level of Catholic dogma I was brainwashed with
for decades, (*and despite the fact that an entire level of Heaven could be
suddenly wiped out with the stroke of a cleric's pen*), I thought I was immune
to death. Exempt. Special. I never thought about death being the natural
order of things. Does anybody? Don't we all want to avoid thinking about
our inevitable end? Our nothingness. Our demise.

After all, I'd tell myself, *Mom lived to be 96. Dad 95. I've got a long, long
time before anything gets me.*

And so I went along, doing as I pleased. Feeling I was invulnerable.
Living in a dream world. I was forty-two years old and at the top of my
game. Big fancy divorce lawyer in the Big Apple. Divorced myself. On
TV sometimes (*if those divorcing were famous, anyway*) I was brought in
to talk about the technical nature of divorcing. I was an acknowledged
expert in the field. Member of various legal organizations. Important guy.
Happy as a clam.

Until the Big C.

I wasn't supposed to get cancer. As far as I could determine, it had only killed one of my relatives—a woman, at that. My Aunt Dora died of ovarian cancer. But I was hardly worried about *that* form of the disease. Or *any* form of the disease.

I was supposed to die of old age. Or a stroke. Or heart disease. Or a car accident. Or a plane crash. Or complications from diabetes. Or screwing some supermodel in her fancy Manhattan digs. But cancer?

"Not in the cards," I used to tell my wife Marion with a smirk—when she *was* still my wife. "People in my family die of heart disease, not cancer."

Imagine the irony when I was diagnosed with esophageal cancer. The kind that eventually killed Roger Ebert. Only I was not going to have the time to write cookbooks like Roger did, well past the point when I could actually physically eat. Nor was I going to allow doctors to disfigure me, take my vocal cords and feed me through tubes in my stomach. None of that for me.

I'd smoked cigars and cigarettes in my youth. The doctors thought my three-pack a day habit might have something to do with my illness. (*You think?*) Still, cancer, a malicious, berserk, exuberant killer, would take me down as I was: standing erect. I would not be reduced to a slobbering, blithering idiot before it got me. I would not be hooked up to machines in the hospital—machines that suctioned out green stuff and made it look like I was having a very bad day at the dentist's office. Nope. I was going to think about how I wanted to go out and plan for it. Develop a mind-set. If I *did* go away from existing on the planet that was the way I *would* go out.

They tell you that cancer knows no rules. It's amoral. Cancer's sole purpose is to destroy life. In that respect, it earns the adjective *immoral*, as well. One expert even said that of all diseases that surgeons treat, they like to call Cancer "The Enemy." This being the case, why aren't these do-nothings developing a cure for The Enemy? It's been around a good long time now.   As far as I'm concerned, ANY disease that draws a bead on Yours Truly and tries to kill me is "The Enemy." Cancer has no monopoly on that designation.

It was explained to me that there are just way too many mutations and variants of the disease to really conquer it. In that regard, it's score ten for cancer and zero for the home team.

I remembered how my own dear mother went out: congestive heart failure. Withered. Cadaverous. Unable to swallow. Incontinent. Head rising to try to get one final gasp of air—like a dog after a long run. In effect, drowning in her own fluids. Grim. I had nightmares about that.

"Why can't I die?" she had moaned, just before lapsing into unconsciousness. "Why can't I just die?"

She revealed that she had dreamt about her funeral in the nights leading up to her final unconscious state. The paid help kept spouting on about heaven and meeting up with dear old dad and a lot of other rot to cheer her up. Mom bought into it, because, after all, she was a devout Catholic, not a fallen-away naysayer like me.

Me? I'm an agnostic. I'm from the Show-Me state on this issue. Or maybe I'm just an atheist. All I know is that all that Catholic stuff didn't take. I don't believe in the Pope's mumbo-jumbo. But then again, I don't believe in any other religion's dogma, either, so the Pope shouldn't feel offended.

That puts me at a distinct disadvantage as I look for some hope to cling to in my final hours. There'll be no "Go to the light." I'm not expecting a happy reunion with deceased relatives. Once in the box, I'll be worm food. Except that I don't want to be buried. Cremation, pure and simple. Just fire me up and scatter me to the four winds.

With all hope erased and the myth of death with dignity pretty much gone with the wind of my (*eventual*) ashes, I was left to read hospice literature with phrases like, "Death belongs to the dying and those who love them."

Ri-i-ight.

If I *HAD* someone who loved me, I hope they sure as hell wouldn't be willing me dead. And what about the part where it says (*and I quote*): "Patients can share quality family time and have a meaningful, dignified, peaceful end-of-life experience."

Is that what Mom had? I remembered her screaming, "Help me! Help me! It hurts! It hurts!" and losing control of her bladder as I frantically tried to grab some liquid morphine—or anything else to alleviate her pain.

I remember the hospice workers coming to the house and asking her very uncool things like, "Where do you want to be buried, Mary? What funeral home do you want to be buried from?" Now is *THAT* a proper way to cheer up a sick person? (*Or proper grammar?*) Ask them about whether they want to be revived? Make them select funeral homes while they're still lucid? Really <u>NOT</u> a good idea.

But Mom was a devout Catholic and she had bought into all the rites and rituals. She was even glad when they offered to send a priest to give her Extreme Unction. (*If they still call it that.*)

When they asked me, I remember thinking that if this guy was going to come before noon, I was going to be even unhappier than I already was, if that were possible. (*I'm not an early morning person.*) And, of course: Bingo! He wanted to "minister to me" at eight o'clock in the morning. (*Not happening, Dude. Just move it along.*)

So it was that I ended up in my cramped rabbit warren of an apartment with a black guy named Bernie who made twenty-seven dollars an hour to wipe the drool from my face, make me a sandwich (*while I can still swallow, anyway*), take me to the bathroom, hose me down in the walk-in shower I had installed ($4,000) and hand me pain meds.

Such is life. And death.

I kept reading the hospice worker's literature. It noted, "Hope plays a part in death from the point of view of the physician and the patient."

Well, yes, hope would definitely be useful. I had <u>NO</u> hope. The doctors had even less for my particular ailment, since it was so far advanced when they discovered it. The brochure had this to say about hope: "Hope deals with the expectation of a good that is yet to be, a perception of a future condition in which a desired goal will be achieved."

What bunk! What did it mean by "a good that is yet to be?" My dying is good for whom? Certainly not for *ME*. Maybe it will be good for Marion, my estranged ex-wife, whom I haven't seen in the flesh for over a decade. Maybe it will be good for Marion's two children by her former marriage—kids I raised as my own, only to have them turn their backs on me and side with their mother, once our divorce was finalized.

And what was this mysterious "future condition in which a desired goal will be achieved." Was that a reference to me lying in a casket or taking up space as ashes in an urn? Sheesh. What complete bullshit.

And so I decided that, if death really "belonged to the dying" (*and their loved ones, of whom I apparently had none*), I could be as nasty, sullen and churlish as I wished during the final hours/days/weeks/months that the good doctors at Cedars Sinai told me I had left—which were not nearly enough. [*Trust me on that.*]

I was encouraged, at first, when the doctors actually did hip replacement surgery on me after I fell down some subway steps. If they thought I was going to croak in the next six months, would they bother to fix my hip? No, I told myself.

So, from that I extrapolated that I might as well go ahead and buy that little red sports car I had been faithfully visiting for a year. A Porsche is a Porsche is a Porsche, and I might as well spend my earthly wealth on buying myself a hot car to tool around in while I still felt halfway decent, because I sure as hell wasn't going to leave my money to either one of those two ungrateful bastard offspring of Marion's that I raised for five years, only to have them side with their bitch of a mother.

And who else was there?

No one, was the answer.

I bought a book called *How We Die*. After all, I had been an English major. What did I know about how people die, aside from some pretty dramatic sequences in movies, which I doubted were accurate. Somehow, I don't think the Jimmy Cagney death scene (*"Made it, Ma. Top of the World, Ma!"*) in *White Heat* really qualified as instructive. Or Al Pacino's in *Scarface*. Nor did the later work of actors as diverse as Richard Dreyfuss in *Whose Life Is It, Anyway?* or Javier Bardem in the equally sobering flick, *The Sea Inside* give me any guidelines to judge. Nor did any of the hundreds of bad guys' deaths, killed in your average thriller. All were bogus.

I needed to know what would *really* happen. I wasn't pleased to learn that I'd get smaller and weaker and exhausted. I'd be unable to swallow and perhaps lapse into unconsciousness before I'd croak.

I read the various stages of accepting death by Elisabeth Kubler Ross entitled *On Death and Dying*. It was encouraging to see that Ross had another book entitled *On Life After Death*. And even more encouraging when I realized that she had yet *another* book with the title that said it was "revised."

Had Kubler Ross found a way to beat the man with the scythe? Was there a secret to living longer that she might share with me, the sickie, in one of her three tomes? I bought all three books. I was unhappy to learn that I was supposed to "accept" my inevitable demise. AND I was out $50.

So much for reading up on the subject at hand. Might as well wing it.

Acceptance? Ha! I'm not accepting nothin', lady.

I'm with Edna St. Vincent Millay, who didn't accept the death of loved ones, either. Forget about the fact that the "loved one" in this case was me, myself and I. I was not "accepting" of the Grim Reaper.

And I was going to hold fast to that "don't tread on me" attitude until I was comatose or the other line in the first guy's book came true—the one that promised improved treatment and the possibility of success from innovative approaches to advanced disease (read "cancer") might give hope even to today's cancer patients.

This last bit would have been more encouraging if the blurb on Amazon hadn't misspelled "hope" as "hop." I'm not kidding. All this research and these new developments were supposed to "bring hop to today's cancer patients." That did nothing but make me want my ten bucks back. That sentiment was underscored by the book's inability to use the words "affect" and "effect" correctly in the synopsis. [As an English major who went on to law school, I had *some* standards. It did not appear from the synopsis that this book had been well proofed. Hopefully, the book's content was better than the book's proofing].

So, I'm now officially aiming at being the World's Worst Terminal Cancer Patient, and I don't care. If people couldn't stand me in life, wait till they get a gander at me in death. I'm going to wallow in self-pity (*"Why me! Why? Why me?!"*) and pretty much make Bernie work hard for his $27 an hour.

Not to mention Alice, Claire and John—the other LPNs and nurses who would be sent to my tiny Manhattan rat-hole by the "Home Alone" service that promised at-home care, rather than warehousing the dying in one of those smelly, terminally depressing nursing homes. [*Nobody wants to go there, and anybody who says they do is lying*].

Fortunately for me, after I graduated with the useless English degree and went on to law school at Marion's urging, I'd bought a good policy that promised these poor schmucks would get paid for putting up with my insufferability.

I was determined to be wrathful, railing against the random cruelty visited upon me. And just as sullen as I felt like being, whenever I felt like exercising that particular emotion. Dying was like a Free Pass to do as I wished—if I still could.

After all: I was the guest of honor at my own death. I might as well enjoy it. At some point, I would become unconscious—if the book I had bought was right.

So much for worrying about what people would say about me once I was gone. I'LL BE GONE! Who *CARES* what Bernie says about me when I'm gone. Or Marion—who cleaned me out financially when we divorced. Or either of her two ungrateful brats by her first husband, the ones I raised (*only to have them turn on me*). Wasn't it the Bard who said, "How sharper than a serpent's tongue is an ungrateful child?"

So, I'm now entering the Final Phase of hospice—or so the experts say. I keep reading the books about dying, and I learned, from them, that it was very Victorian of me to think that there wouldn't be a miserable prelude to the final moments of my life. The book said this reassurance that it would be "peaceful" was what everyone wanted to hear.

Well, yes, I could appreciate that. It would be like the time the doctor told me that the shot he was about to sink deep into the bony part of my

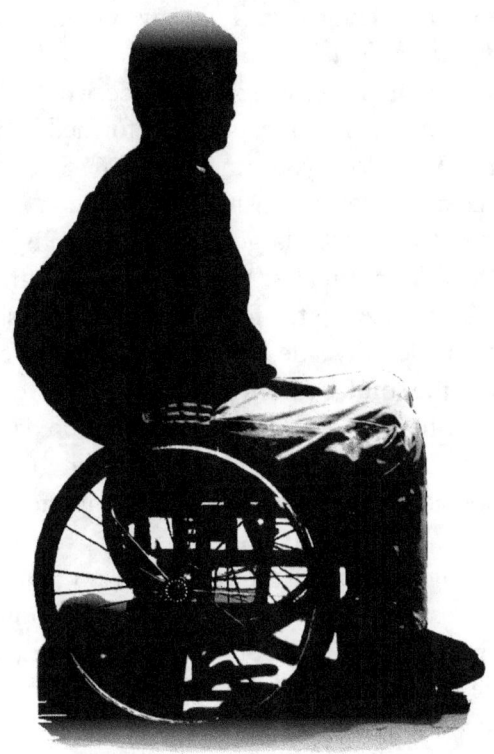

knee wouldn't hurt. (*Indian accent: "Oh, no. This won't hurt."*) It hurt like a son-of-a-bitch. Apparently, this would, too.

Don't we all hope that we'll simply die in our beds one dark night, sleeping away with no pain or suffering? But that isn't how it works out at all, is it, Kids? Don't most of us really, really suffer at the end, one way or another?

Certainly both of my parents had suffered mightily, one with a painful heart attack and one with congestive heart failure. And Marion's parents, when we were still together, had died of Alzheimer's disease and cancer. I was always secretly glad that it was Marion's father who had the cancer, since "my people" didn't *GET* cancer. Ha!

And as for Alzheimer's disease: if there is anything crueler than dementia gone wild, depriving a person of the very personality that made them who they were, taking away their ability to recognize their family members, curling them into the fetal position until their brain forgets to send them the signal to breathe—well, what would it be? *Esophageal cancer, probably, given my luck,* I thought wryly.

But I was still hoping to somehow beat Death at his own game.

Bernie came in at ten o'clock. (*I had given strict orders not to wake me at some ungodly earlier hour*).

"You want I should make you some coffee, Mr. Walters?" Bernie gave me a big smile revealing his large, perfectly formed white teeth.

"No, Bernie. Why don't you run over to 56th Street to Al's and get me a nice, big chocolate milkshake instead."

Bernie looked at me with large, sad eyes. Then he asked, "Really?"

"Yes, really. Why not really? Why should I confine my final days to ordinary coffee? Let's jazz up the festivities here. Let's shake it up a bit!"

And so Bernie left my side, after calling Alice to cover for him, and took a subway to the soft ice cream place I liked over on 56th Street. It was a long way from where I lived, but that was just too damn bad.

When Bernie returned, nearly an hour later, gripping a now-warm and melted chocolate milkshake in a paper container, I said, "Better late than never."

He didn't laugh. Funny. I thought of all my "dedicated caregivers," Bernie had the best shot at possessing a sense of humor. Apparently his sense of humor didn't extend to a one-hour subway trip across town to get me a milkshake, followed by absolutely no thanks from the patient.

As the days dragged by and I was still among the living, I became more and more demanding.

"Alice," I said when the portly middle-aged woman arrived for her two to six shift, "why don't you cut my toenails?"

Alice gave me a look that could best be described as withering, but she dutifully got out the manicure set. She was not a young woman. She had to sit on a small stool at my feet in order to wield the small implement.

My nails were nasty: all yellow and thick and old looking. This was unusual for someone not yet out of their forties, but I figured Alice would have seen plenty of old geezers with the same sort of toenails. Maybe some of them even had gout.

As soon as Alice tried to trim the first toenail, she nicked me. She wore thick glasses. I don't think her eyesight was the best amongst my four caretakers.

"Jesus, Alice! Take it easy, will you? I may not be around long enough to run the Boston Marathon, but unless you want to have to carry me to the john on your back, try to leave me two feet that work." I harrumphed a bit deriding the stout woman.

Alice didn't say anything at first. Then, she said, "I'm sorry, Mr. Walters. I didn't mean to nick you. I'll be more careful."

THAT was more like it.

When Claire and John arrived for their respective shifts, I was just as difficult, testy and unpleasant. It came quite naturally, I must say. I'd been on my best behavior for so long that it was nice to finally let my hair down and be the *real* me.

The real me was in a bad place, and I didn't care who knew it.

The other caretakers—John, Claire and Bernie—got their fair share of ill treatment, also. And my illness dragged on. And on. And on.

Days become weeks and weeks became months.

Thankfully, for me, the economy had tanked in 2008, so all of the RNs and LPNs employed by "Home Alone" needed their jobs. There would be no quitting, no matter how surly or churlish I became.

Still, I noticed that, as each shift handed off to the next, there was more and more whispered conversation amongst the caretaker handing the torch off to the next victim.

And then came the night when Claire—who had the thinnest skin of the bunch and burst into tears at one of my outbursts—came at me with a syringe, telling me it was "just something to help you sleep."

It helped me sleep, all right. Permanently.

Circle Six: Heresy

The Final Victim

Lee had been drinking since late afternoon. It didn't so much stop the pain of the voices in his head, as clarify what the voices were saying.

I'll do the Reverend's bidding, to a point, thought Lee. *Reverend Jones says Dave Downing has to die. If God or the devil wants poor old Dave dead, He must give me some sort of sign. I ain't no cold-blooded killer!*

Lee took another swig of Old Milwaukee. He would have preferred Jack Daniels, but he didn't have the money.

Lee looked out the window of the shabby white house that stood below the hill. High up on the hill was where the rich people lived. The poor people lived down here. Lee was staring at the wet grass of his small yard. It had rained less than an hour ago. He thought the drops of water on the grass resembled the tears of some gigantic creature.

Lee popped the top of his sixth beer and glanced outside again.

Suddenly, birds. Thousands and thousands of birds. Black birds. European starlings. They were everywhere! On his lawn. On the lawn of the neighbor to his left, Ed Grant. On Rose Till's lawn, his neighbor to the right. He watched Rosie Till's golden collie, Honey, barking furiously as she chased the birds as far as her chain would allow.

"Melanie! Come quick! There's birds everywhere! They're peckin' away at our yard and Ed's and Rosie's."

Melanie Elliot rushed down the stairs. She could hear the urgency in her husband's drunken voice. She stared in astonishment at the spectacle taking place outside on their lawn.

"The weird thing is that the birds stop right there," she said, pointing to the perimeter of their neighbors' lawns. Melanie was right. The birds were covering nearly every inch of Lee's lawn and Ed's lawn and Rose's lawn. But the ubiquitous birds, clucking and pecking and sucking eagerly at the earth's bosom, stopped at the sidewalks of the two neighboring houses. Only three lawns were infested by the omnipresent birds.

There were no birds across the street. There were no birds on any other lawns beyond those three, which they could see by glancing up and down Third Street. Only here, in their lawn and those of their two closest neighbors, were there hundreds—thousands, even—of noisy, hungry, pecking black birds, greedily digging with their beaks. But what were they digging for?

Melanie asked the question, "What do you think they're eating? What are they looking for, Lee?" She asked, "Are they migrating? Is there some special food in just these three lawns that they've targeted? It's so weird that they aren't across the street or, really, anywhere but on these three lawns." She shook her head in confusion.

Lee took a deep breath. He had just realized something that gave him a start. He was going to have to admit to the Reverend that he had been given a sign. The Reverend Jeremiah Jones had predicted to Lee just yesterday that he would be given a sign—a sign that he must follow Reverend Jeremiah Jones' instructions.

Jeremiah said to Lee, "The heavens might open up. You might hear a loud voice telling you to do what I tell you. To do what is necessary. It has to be the way I tell you. You'll have to follow my directions. To the letter." The Reverend spoke slowly, in a stern tone of voice.

Lee thought, *This must be the sign the Reverend was talking about. What else could it be?*

What Lee and Melanie Elliot were seeing defied logic. There was no reasonable explanation for the sudden appearance of hordes of angry black birds, mimicking Alfred Hitchcock's movie *The Birds.*

The small black creatures were everywhere: on the gables of the houses. On the roofs of Lee's house and his neighbors' homes. On their lawns. In the trees. Greedily pecking at the still-wet grass, searching for some mysterious food item. Some magic worm, perhaps? The entire experience left both Lee and Melody chattering about the occurrence with their next-door neighbors for hours afterwards. No one knew of any logical explanation.

But Lee thought he might know what it all meant. And he didn't like what it meant for his future.

Reverend Jeremiah Jones lived in the dilapidated trailer court across from the high school. It was a seedy, run-down place. The road in and out was so rutted, filled with such deep potholes, that you were best advised to park your car at the gate in the combined Laundromat Seven-Eleven parking lot, and walk in. The Reverend kept a dog on a chain outside his trailer. The Reverend told Lee the dog tethered outside was "for protection."

When Lee asked Reverend Jones, "Why do you need protection? What do you need protection from? And how would a dog help?" the Reverend gave him a sideways glance, smiled an enigmatic half-smile, and said, "Why, protection from God, of course."

"Why do you need protection from God? And why use a dog?" asked Lee, genuinely puzzled.

Jeremiah said, "You've read about or heard of Cerberus, the three-headed Hound of Hell, haven't you?"

Lee didn't want to admit that he couldn't read. He had dropped out of his special education classes in eighth grade. He did remember that the smart kids in Mrs. Watson's class were reading a Myths and Legends unit, using the large, brown book most students in her eighth grade classroom used.

Lee was not issued one of those books. He had a green book, instead. But Lee could hear the students who were issued the brown literature book reading some of the stories in it aloud and discussing them.

Lee was assigned the green book for junior high school students who were two grade levels or more behind: *Open Highways*, it was called. The other students were reading from a completely different series, *Great Literature of the World*. Lee could only listen as the others around him dis-

cussed the myths of Persephone and Narcissus and Hercules and Cerberus and other long words describing gods and goddesses—names with many syllables that Lee would never have been able to pronounce or remember, even if he could read.

Mrs. Watson had summoned reading experts from the teaching university, Western Illinois University, in Macomb, Illinois, to try to help Lee learn to read. That didn't happen until all other avenues were exhausted. The subjects, themselves (*Lee and his teacher*), were exhausted.

She worked with Lee, one-on-one, many nights after school as he tried his best to make sense of the words. But the letters were always all mixed up. Sometimes, the letters were backwards. If there was a picture on the page, sometimes Lee could guess at the meaning of the word, but the letters, themselves, were as useless in conveying meaning to Lee and as mysterious as the marauding birds on his lawn. Often, he'd have trouble concentrating, because the voices in his head would become too loud.

I'm not going to tell a smart guy like Jeremiah Jones that I can't read good, Lee thought. *I'll just nod my head. Pretend I know what he's talking about.*

The Reverend eyed the much-younger man with cool curiosity. Jeremiah had the flat stare of a cat looking at its master while ignoring his master, as usual.

It was about that time that the Reverend Jones took Lee into the attached lean-to next to his trailer and showed Lee the knives and other weapons. A crudely-drawn pentagram dominated the small room. It appeared to have been drawn in red paint on the floor of the hastily-constructed lean-to structure. (*Only later did Lee learn what the true composition of the pentagram paint was.*)

"This is where it happens," the Reverend Jones said to Lee, solemnly indicating the seedy shack.

"Where what happens?" Lee asked. He was almost afraid to hear the answer.

"The sacrifices."

"Sacrifices? Sacrifices for what? What do you sacrifice? And why?"

"The sacrifices are to keep Lucifer happy. He is powerful, you know. As powerful as God. I sacrifice small things to Him. Lucifer was the most powerful angel in heaven, until He fell from favor. Why, His very name means 'light bringing' or 'the morning star.' See that planet over there?"

Jones pointed to a bright constantly glittering globe giving off a steady light visible in the night sky.

"Yeah. So what?" asked Lee.

"That's Venus, Lucifer's special planet. Trust me, Lucifer was—IS—just as important as God ever was. These sacrifices will help Lucifer regain his position and His power. But I have to follow His instructions and do as He commands, sacrificing whatever He requires. I must make that happen. You have to help me. I can't do it alone."

Jones spat a brown stream of chewing tobacco at the small dog on the chain tethered outside his ramshackle trailer. The dog looked grateful for the attention. It yipped a few times. Any attention—even negative attention—was preferable to being completely invisible. Lee could attest to that.

"He *ASKS* you to do this?" Lee stammered.

"Yes. Of course. You hear voices, too, don't you?"

Lee looked closely at the Reverend.

How does he know? Did I tell him I heard voices in my head when I was drunk? How does Reverend Jones know that I hear voices telling me to do things? That I've BEEN hearing them for a very long time?

But Lee resisted the voices. He hadn't sacrificed Rose's dog, Honey, like the voices told him to. He'd fought back, telling himself that he was a good person.

Good people don't go around murdering their neighbor's dog, even if the dog is annoying. Good people don't hear voices that tell them to do bad things. Melanie thinks I'm a good person. I'm going to try to be a good person for her.

But now the Reverend Jeremiah Jones was staring at Lee. He was giving him an odd look. It was a look that said, *I know who you are. You are my disciple. You WILL do my bidding.*

Eventually, in fact, the Reverend Jones uttered that very thought aloud. He told Lee that he, Lee Elliot must help the Reverend in his mission. And the Reverend's mission was to aid Lucifer in regaining His power. The Reverend wanted to help Lucifer once again rule the world.

"There's also money in it for you, Lee—if you do it right, and don't get caught," Jeremiah said.

"Do what right?"

Lee was more than a little afraid of the creepy look, the somber demeanor, the sepulchral tone in the Reverend's voice. Even though it was daylight outside, inside the tiny little hut where they were standing, the shed guarded by Jeremiah's dog, it was pitch black. There were no windows. The walls had been soundproofed—no doubt to keep the neighbors from hearing the dying screams of the sacrificial animals Jeremiah said he always sacrificed on this very spot. There was a musty, unpleasant odor in the closed room. Lee just wanted to get out of there. The sooner, the better.

"We need a bigger sacrifice," Jeremiah continued. "The biggest one yet. A man. This sacrifice will make us both rich and enhance us in the eyes of Lucifer." Jeremiah's eyes were glittering madly as he began to recite George Meredith: "On a starred night Prince Lucifer arose, Tired of his dark dominion, swung the fiend above the rolling ball in cloud part screened."

"What are you talking about?" Lee asked, backing away.

"You know about Lucifer from reading your Bible, don't you, Lee?" Jeremiah asked.

Once again, Lee felt inferior. Dumb. Illiterate. But he wasn't going to answer the question and let the Reverend know his secret. The Reverend had always treated Lee as an equal. That was something Lee had not been accustomed to in school.

Lee had always been looked down upon as a member of "the dumb group," the seven ones (7-1) or seven twos (7-2). The smart kids were in the seven fives (7-5). The average kids were in the seven threes (7-3) and seven fours (7-4). Lee was labeled dysfunctional. Special education. He was treated as such by association with the other students in his class of seven ones, a school section designation. His I.Q. was determined to be 70—well below the normal average of 100.

At twenty-five, over ten years out of school, Lee just wanted to appear normal. He wanted to be like all the rest of his classmates. He wanted to be accepted. Get a job. Find a wife. Have some kids. But Lee constantly ran into brick walls. His inability to read dogged him. His failure to go past eighth grade and graduate from either junior high school or high school marked him as someone who would never hold more than a menial job. Which was what he had now: a job as a janitor in the Woolworth's store on the corner downtown, right next to the library. He swept up and made minimum wage. He had found a good woman in Melanie, but they didn't have enough money to get married or have kids. They only had the house because it had been Melanie's parents. She inherited it in their will when they died in a car accident. It was all they could do to pay the taxes on the ramshackle dwelling.

Peering intently into Lee's eyes, the Reverend articulated his plan for world dominion. Lucifer would help them both. Lee would be the Reverend's second-in-command. The riches they would reap would be put to good use and benefit both of them and the fallen angel.

Lee backed out of the smelly, dark room. The close coppery smell reminded of blood and entrails. He was skeptical. Lee objected, again, aloud, "I need a sign. I need some sort of sign. I need to know that you're not just making all this stuff up."

"You'll have your sign. The heavens will give you a sign," Jeremiah had said, smiling in a smug, self-satisfied way. It was then that the Reverend told him about David Downing. Jeremiah told Lee the rumor was that David Downing kept a large amount of cash in his wooden leg.

David only had one leg. He lost his right leg in Korea when a mine exploded. It was replaced with a primitive wooden peg leg—all that was available to someone of limited means. Dave was a short, unhealthy, fifty-five-year-old man—a man who had never done anything bad to Lee Elliot. Or, as far as Lee knew, to Jeremiah Jones.

Why Dave? Why does it have to be Dave Downing? Lee thought.

Lee agonized. If David hadn't been overly nice to Lee, at least he had not called him any of the derogatory names his classmates used to call him: moron, imbecile, idiot. Dave had not suggested that Lee Elliot was stupid or slow. Dave had treated him fair and square. For this, Lee was grateful. Lee didn't like the thought that he was being asked to harm someone who had never done any harm to him (*Lucifer or no Lucifer.*) He needed a sign. And it had better be a damn good one!

Reverend Jones sat Lee down on a straight-back chair and explained for the second time why Dave was the perfect human sacrifice.

"Dave's wooden leg has money in it. Lots and lots of money. We need that money to insure that we succeed in helping restore Lucifer to His former position of power. I want you to kill Dave Downing. Throw his body in a ditch. Remove his peg leg. Bring that peg leg with the cash in it back here. The peg leg will be proof that you have succeeded. We'll split the money. No more Old Milwaukee for you, Lee. You can buy yourself some real whiskey. Or at least a better brand of beer."

Jeremiah smiled a snaggle-toothed, brown smile.

"Take this knife." Jeremiah handed Lee a blade at least ten inches long. It was a lethal-looking butcher knife. "You might need it for after, to remove the leg. You'll definitely need it when you kill him—unless you want to strangle him." Jeremiah said all this matter-of-factly, as though they were discussing a simple haircut, not a fatal stabbing or death by strangulation. "After you're done, throw it in the Rock River. You should drive right over the bridge on your way home."

Lee couldn't imagine holding his hands on another human being's windpipe, throttling them in a death grip until they died. It sounded even more gruesome than using the knife. So he took the large, ten-inch blade from the Reverend's vast array of weapons.

Lee Elliot shivered and stammered out his latest excuse.

"I've got to get home. Melanie's expecting me for supper. I need some time to think about this. I still need some kind of sign. Something to confirm what you've said."

The Reverend just nodded his head sagely. He said, "You'll have your sign. Never fear. When you have it, you must act."

That had been yesterday. Before the birds came.

When Dave Downing left the Thirsty Shamrock on his way home on Friday night, Lee Elliot stood in the shadows of the alley, waiting for him. Lee was shivering both with the cold of the April night and with fear. Lee had never killed anything bigger than a squirrel. His daddy never let him go hunting with the other boys in the Elliot family. Lee heard his father say once, to Lee's mom, "He's so dumb, he'll probably just shoot his fool foot off!"

Lee thought that an ironic statement now, in light of what he was about to do, although the term "ironic" would not have been one Lee could define. That sort of vocabulary was absent from Lee's eighth grade education. Lee had been held back so many times that he drove himself to school in eighth grade. It was time for him to quit. Even his parents agreed. He dropped out at the end of the first semester of his eighth grade year. It didn't look like the school was going to okay his graduation with his class, anyway. That would have been just one more humiliation in a long line of them.

"You don't want to be the oldest kid in the ninth grade, do you?" his parents told him. "You're already sixteen years old and driving. You passed your driver's test, didn't you? Enough of this school nonsense. It's not working for you, Boy. Quit and get a job."

With that pronouncement from Buddy Elliot, Lee's father, Lee's formal education was over. Lee was on his own, and the road ahead would be rocky, indeed. Jobs for students with a seventh grade education were not plentiful. Lee began a long, painful spiral towards feeling even worse about himself than he had when in school.

The only bright spot in his life, until he met Melanie, was being hired to mop floors at the local Walgreen's. After that, Melanie provided companionship, but she was constantly on his case about needing to make more money for the taxes on the house and for everything else. Melanie wanted to have a child. They could barely live on what the two of them made (*Melanie worked at McDonald's*). How could they afford a child?

But, Lee thought, *if the Reverend is right about the money in Dave Downing's leg, that could change everything.* David Downing's pathetic excuse for a prosthetic leg began to loom as second only to the lottery as the way out of their miserable existence.

It had been while attending one of the Reverend Jeremiah Jones' revival meetings, down by the Mississippi River on River Drive last spring, that Lee first felt a flush of acceptance in the real world. The Reverend didn't treat him like he was impaired. He didn't call him "stupid" or any of the mean things that Lee's classmates and even Lee's own father called him.

The Reverend, in fact, always spoke to Lee as though Lee were his equal, alluding to things that Lee couldn't follow as conversational topics, since Lee's inability to read and his lack of formal education dogged him at every step—even socially. When Jeremiah mentioned Cerberus or reading the Bible, the Reverend acted as though he thought Lee was capable of following what he said. He treated Lee as though he actually might have read these great works. He never once treated Lee as incompetent or dumb. Far from it. The Reverend treated Lee much better than Lee's own parents, siblings, and classmates had ever treated him.

Lee soon decided that he'd stick by the Reverend as long as the Reverend would have him for a friend. And, too, Lee's Uncle Karl Elliot was the minister of Kewanee's Lutheran Church of the Redeemer. Lee's Dad,

Bud, had always been very proud of this family connection to his older brother. Religion was a good thing in the Elliot household. It was a good thing that none of them knew exactly the type of religion the Reverend Jeremiah Jones practiced. The Reverend kept his true beliefs hidden behind more conventional public professions of faith at his tent revival meetings, where he raised donations, which he lived on.

That was how and why Lee ended up spending long hours in the Reverend Jeremiah Jones' company. That was how and why Lee learned the secret of the shoddy shack behind the Reverend's trailer and what it was *really* used for. That was how and why Lee ended up in a dark alley behind the Thirsty Shamrock bar, waiting in the shadows for a crippled man to emerge and hobble down the alley to his Ford pick-up, after which he would drive his pick-up truck towards the small house where David Downing, Korean War veteran, lived alone.

Lee didn't kill Dave in the alley. He approached the older man and asked for a favor.

"Can I get a ride home, Dave?"

Lee and Dave knew each other from the bingo hall, the Reverend's tented revival meetings, and the VFW (Veterans of Foreign Wars). Lee's daddy, Buddy, was also a veteran. The two sometimes drank together in the dark bar of the low-slung brown building located across the street from the police station. They both lived out Colona way, in the country.

"Sure, Lee," Dave said, hoisting his crippled form behind the wheel of the small Ford pick-up truck. Dave had a specially designed, custom-fitted accelerator pedal, for use with his wooden leg. He braked with his normal left leg and accelerated with his right peg leg firmly inserted in a circular hole made especially for that purpose. As long as he didn't have to walk long distances, Dave Downing got around just fine.

As they drove towards the farm in Colona where Lee lived, they would pass across railroad tracks, a bridge over the Rock River, and continue for several miles on the sub-road that, otherwise, would lead to Interstate 80. If you kept going far enough, you'd come to the brand-new winery where John Boehner had come to raise money for a Republican Tea Party candidate in August of 2014. But Lee didn't plan to let Dave drive that far.

Once they left behind the few occupied homes on the gravel road, Lee said, "I have to pee, Dave. Can you pull over?"

"Can't you hold it, Lee?" Dave asked. He seemed miffed that he was giving the kid a ride home, and now he would have to stop to allow him to urinate in the ditch.

"Sorry, Dave. I had one too many Old Milwaukees, I guess. I'm afraid I'll piss in your truck if you don't pull over." Lee looked appropriately sheepish and apologetic.

Hearing that, Dave hurriedly pulled over next to a ditch with tall grass and weeds in abundance. No houses anywhere in sight. The only light this night seemed to come from a large full moon and an unusually bright light from Lucifer's planet, Venus.

Lee acted as though he were reaching for the door handle of the ancient Ford truck. Instead, he pulled the large blade the Reverend had given him from beneath his jacket.

Lee and Jeremiah had discussed the best way to dispatch prey as large as David Downing. Jeremiah had much more experience in killing things. He had sacrificed stray dogs as large as one hundred pounds. Jeremiah had advised Lee, "Slit his throat, Lee. It'll be messy, yes, but he'll bleed out faster if you slash him straight across the jugular vein and the carotid artery. Take his body and remove the leg. Cut it off, if you have to. Bring the peg leg here. Throw his body in a ditch where no one will see you do it. Dump the knife in the Rock River. Take his truck, but when you finally abandon it, wipe it down for fingerprints. Can you remember all that?"

Jeremiah looked dubiously at Lee, wondering if Lee had the intelligence and chutzpah to pull this off. The Reverend had been grooming Lee for this for months now. The lucky coincidence of the migrating European starlings had given Jeremiah the perfect opportunity to prey on the ignorance and naiveté of this child-man. Jeremiah could hardly believe his good fortune when the poor boy had stumbled into his tent that warm June night, following his mother, Cassie. Jeremiah knew right away that he had found his patsy.

The knife sliced through Dave's neck so cleanly that Dave didn't even cry out. The blood spray from the violence splashed on the interior of the windshield. On Dave's clothes. On Lee's clothes. All over the inside of the truck. Lee walked around the outside of the truck to the driver's side. He pulled Dave Downing's limp body from the truck. Dave was still making a gurgling sound. He put up little fight before lapsing into unconsciousness, hands clutching at his hemorrhaging neck. The decorated veteran had been taken completely by surprise.

Lee dragged Dave's body to the ditch. He threw him headfirst into its depths. There was a small amount of water in the bottom of the four-foot ditch. It was into this blackish murk that Lee plunged after his prey, carrying out the plan to remove Dave's fake right leg. The leg came off easily. Lee did not have to use the knife again. He was grateful for that. Lee tried to rinse his blood-soaked hands and face in the black water.

Lee was breathing heavily. He was splattered with blood. His heart was pounding so loudly in his chest that he was certain it could be heard miles away. Lee heard a voice in his head shouting, "YOU KILLED HIM! YOU KILLED HIM! YOU KILLED HIM!" The voice was louder than those he routinely heard, but the message was a recrimination. The voice didn't say it, but Lee felt as though the voice would soon add, "YOU STUPID IDIOT! YOU STUPID IDIOT! YOU STUPID IDIOT!"

When Lee had Dave's peg leg firmly in his bloody grasp, he expected to find green bills spilling forth from the truncated area where the peg leg had been attached. But there was nothing in the leg. Nothing concealed under the leg, either. This surprised Lee, as Jeremiah had painted a picture of large amounts of cash that the veteran would have secreted inside his wooden leg.

Lee threw the peg leg into the truck bed. He climbed behind the wheel, glancing furtively to his left and right, looking for the tell-tale sign of a tail-light heading away or headlights coming towards him. Lee was feeling guilty and he was feeling queasy. The voice in his head kept screaming, "YOU KILLED HIM! YOU KILLED HIM!" Lee just wanted the voice to stop.

He drove off in Dave's truck, heading for Reverend Jeremiah Jones' trailer, the useless wooden peg leg making a hollow tumbling noise in the empty bed of the truck, like a bird hitting a glass window. It sounded like a heavy object tumbling inside a package. It was a sound like a tennis shoe tumbling in the dryer, only with sharper percussions.

When he reached the trailer park, Lee parked under a large tree near the Laundromat just at the entrance of Happy Hollow Trailer Park. He grabbed the peg leg from the bed of the truck, tucked it under his jacket so no one would see what he was carrying, and began walking towards the Reverend's plot. This was part of the plan. Jeremiah had explained to Lee that it wouldn't do for them to be seen together. He wanted Lee to make sure he wasn't followed and to come to his trailer on foot, using the back way. Lee did all this, as requested.

Upon reaching the entrance to the shabby trailer, Lee knocked on the door. He knocked a second time, more loudly. Lee was standing near the entrance to the attached Sacrificial Shed, as Jeremiah referred to the wooden shanty nearby. Lee thought he heard a noise coming from within. It was a faint sound, no doubt muffled by the sound-proofing. It sounded like a bleating animal. Lee turned away from the trailer door and moved towards the doorway of the nearby Sacrificial Shed. It was slightly ajar.

Within, he saw the specter of Jeremiah Jones, knife raised. A terrified creature, approximately three feet high, eyes glazed with fear, helpless, was tied in front of the Reverend. It was a small goat, immobilized by ropes. Jeremiah brought the axe-like weapon down on the animal's head just as Lee opened the door to enter.

Jeremiah was breathing heavily from his exertions. The struggling wounded goat was bleeding and making a horrible noise in its death throes, still pinioned at the Reverend's feet. Jeremiah Jones looked up at Lee Elliot and smiled the evil smile of an ogre. The grin of a conscienceless monster. The smirk of a manipulative Machiavelli.

"Did you bring his leg?" Jeremiah asked.

Lee shook his head yes. He reached beneath his jacket to pull forth Dave Downing's prosthesis.

Jeremiah glanced at the leg. He looked up at Lee, stepping over the still struggling dying creature to come closer to Lee, bloody axe still in his hand.

"Where's the money?" the Reverend asked.

"There wasn't any," said Lee.

"What? No money? There HAS to be. You took the cash, didn't you?" Jeremiah screamed.

"No, Sir," replied Lee. "There wasn't any money. I killed Dave just the way you said to. I threw his body in a ditch out past Colona. Out near Interstate 80. I took his leg off. But there wasn't anything inside it."

"LIAR!" screamed the enraged minister as he lunged at the timid young man, bloody axe raised. "Stupid fucking liar! You took it, didn't you? You took the money! Where is it? Give it to me!"

The Reverend Jeremiah Jones approached Lee with menace in his manner and murder in his heart.

In that moment, Lee Elliot wished he had brought the large butcher knife with him. But Lee had done as the Reverend Jones had instructed. He had thrown the knife into the raging Rock River, which was at near-flood levels this wet spring. Lee had no weapon. Nor had he thought he would need one.

The man he had trusted and aided in committing the most heinous act of his life was about to betray him. Almost the last thing Lee Elliot saw was also the last thing the goat had seen: a heavy axe-like weapon descending on his skull. Coming down so quickly and so forcefully that Lee had no time to fend it off.

As the weapon found its mark, Lee heard birds twittering. He was not sure if he was once again seeing the birds of Lucifer's sign to him—the European starlings on his front lawn that day—or if neurons were firing stored memories in his head in death. With that last mortal impression of flocks of black birds tearing at the ground, ripping apart the blades of grass, laying waste to everything they touched, Lee Elliot became just one more in a long string of the Reverend Jeremiah Jones' sacrifices.

The Reverend stood above him, bloody axe poised to strike again, muttering, "You moron. Lucifer always meant for you to be the final victim."

Circle Seven:
The Violent

KILLAL

Q *ICUSR*
Alex looked over the letters on his "Hanging with Friends" board. The letters were arrayed on the screen of his Android 3G phone like letters on a Scrabble game tile board.

He checked the letters for point value. Q was tops: ten points. "K" was worth five points.

Rats! Too many "L's." An "L" is only two points.

He smiled, thinking about the word he was about to send to the opponent randomly chosen by his phone, WitchyWoman.

Better be "quick", if I use this one, Witchy. Wonder if you'll get it?

Alex hadn't entered the word yet. He always tried for the word with the highest point total. If you didn't have points in the bank—at least twenty points—you couldn't use the two "help" functions. (Not that they really "helped" that much.)

One—the blue button on the far left—gave you four letters that might be in the word you were solving. Three of them were wrong answers. If it was a long word, you only had a ridiculously few chances to guess it. The red fireplug button in the middle would eliminate four letters automatically.

Alex hated guessing long words that filled the entire 8-letter slate. He disliked the minimum-length 4-letter ones that could be any of ten different choices almost as much. Last time he played *Witchy*, she used BODE. By the time Alex got to the point of being able to guess the first letter, he only had two chances left: CODE or RODE. He usually guessed wrong. The last of his five balloons burst. His avatar—the little man clutching five balloons—fell into the molten lava with a horrified look on his face. Alex lost.

Alex hated to lose. An alpha male hates being bested. Alex had anger issues. But his psychiatrist said he was making progress.

As balloon man sank into the volcano, Alex thought, *Shit! That sucks!!*

Half the time, Alex was sure that Witchy was just jerking his chain. She didn't know the meanings of the words she sent him. *ZARF? No way. ZEBUS? R-i-i-i-g-h-t.*. Witchy just filled in letters. She hoped the game would take them when she pressed "submit". Sometimes, it did. Sometimes, it didn't.

Putting in random letters isn't fair. He took another sip of the gin and tonic he had settled down with this evening to play catch up in these word games with his "friends." Alex enjoyed a good stiff drink now and again. This ritual was becoming one of his favorites.

Alex would admit that he might be obsessive compulsive. Fairness. He believed in fairness. He hated bullies and anyone who, given a little power, loved to lord it over others. Cops. Administrators. Company CEOs. George W. Bush. Alex was a fighter. He would stand up for himself. All his friends knew that. Most of his enemies, too. The way Alex figured, that just made him a valuable ally. Alex would stand up for his friends, too. He'd stand up to anybody—if he had to.

Sometimes, I get a little strident. A little over-the-top. But I'm getting better. Dr. Geifman says so. That DUI arrest was a good thing for me. I didn't

handle that very well, but I'm better now. That wouldn't happen today. I'd handle it better.

Alex had heard there was an app you could get for Hanging with Friends. It would give you all the possible words that you could form from your slate of letters. Alex wouldn't stoop to such tricks.

"It isn't fair," he had told his racquetball partner, Randy. Alex would beat Witchy fair and square.

I'm not going to cheat to win. I want to win fair and square. Oooooh! "Square" would be a hard one! Can I make SQUARE? Damn! No "A." Next time.

He pushed shuffle. It was only then, as the letters rearranged themselves, that he noticed that the top line contained two real words: **KILLAL.**

Too bad I can't use a compound word command like that, he thought. *Should say KILLBILL, like that movie with Uma Thurman. Oh, wait. Too many letters. Maybe FUKOFF.*

Alex smiled.

Compound words were fair game, of course. Once, Alex made "EAR-WAX." Another time, he played "EYEBALL." "HOTRODS." (That one had been too easy; you shouldn't repeat the same letter. The opponent would be given all the "O's.")

The game only took eight letter words. It was essentially a guessing game. An educated guessing game. You guessed what word your friend had made and sent you, electronically. You responded with a word of your own from the twelve letters sent you electronically. Once your five balloons popped, you fell into the lava pit. And, as Porky Pig used to say, "Th-th-th-that's all, Folks."

Alex had been obsessively playing "Hanging with Friends," a Zynga game, on his Android 3G phone for months now. He started playing during his time in the anger management clinic in Minneapolis, to kill time. He had exhausted all competitors he knew in real life. Now he was letting the phone select opponents for him. He had no idea how his Android 3G phone found competitors. He didn't know WitchyWoman IRL.

The phone had also selected another opponent, Zyrgfwat. Zyrgfwat was kind of a wash. He seldom guessed any of the words Alex sent. Zyrgfwat didn't send very difficult words, either. *The man must be a moron,* Alex thought. Zyrgfwat seemed a bit of a dullard. He did not seem to know anything about letter digraphs like "sh" or "ch." *Oh, well, better for me,* Alex thought.

But the level of competitive play was much higher with WitchyWoman. He looked forward to their matches.

Alex was a good player. One of the best. He beat his opponents so often that many of them "resigned." They simply quit playing. But not Witchy. Witchy sometimes won. Alex looked over the words he had made and was waiting for opponents to respond to: SHAMAN, QUEANS, PYEMIA, ZARF, again. [*Hey! Why stop when you've got a winner?*] KNIVES. He thought there was a word CWTH that didn't even use a vowel. He just hadn't tried that one yet.

Probably the machine won't take it. It takes CROCS and ZITS, which are way too slangy, but it probably won't take that perfectly respectable crossword answer.

Alex liked knowing the gender of his opponent.

I don't really know that Zyrgfwat isn't female. Wonder why I just automatically assume that Zyrgfwat is male? Maybe because he makes such dumb guesses. Alex enjoyed another quick sip of his gin and tonic. He'd made it too strong. The lime had slipped to the bottom of the glass so he couldn't squeeze it into the liquid without submerging nearly all his fingers into the drink. Not good.

Alex's phone sent a message that the battery was low. It must be attached to an outside power source. He glanced at the top line choices before selecting "QUICK" as his word.

Yeah. Right. I don't even KNOW an Al. Sorry.

Alex put the phone away until he could recharge the battery. It didn't matter. The opponents needed time to respond. Sometimes it took days. He'd been waiting for Scott43 to solve QUARK for 32 days. But Alex was self-employed. He worked from home. He could play as much or as little as he wanted. Whenever. Wherever. He found himself devoting more and more time to Zynga's "Hanging with Friends."

And WitchyWoman was his primary competition.

After dinner (a period of time during which Alex was able to recharge his cell phone), he fired up the Android again.

WitchyWoman had responded. He clicked to view her attempt to solve "QUICK" as the machine commanded him to do. The final vowel, the letter "I" was always given to the player. Witchy was quick (*Alex smiled*). She selected "U" as her next guess.

And if there's a "U," can a "Q" be far behind? he thought.

In just seconds, WitchyWoman had solved the word, with six of seven strikes left.

Now, it was WitchyWoman's turn to send Alex a word.

BUREAU.

Alex got it, but it took him a while. The new tiles for the word he was to make flashed on his screen.

Bottom line: **KILLAL.** Top line: **SMAVRO**

Odd. It said "KILLAL" on the top line 3 games back. Wonder what the problem is?

After pushing the "shuffle" button, Alex made the word SKILL.

Ten games later, eight of which Alex won, he had received the letters KILLAL five times. Not always in sequence, of course, but the letters were always there. Something was wrong with his phone. Or with the game. Time to send an E-mail to Zynga.

Alex googled Zynga. He found customer service. He scribbled the address and phone number on a scrap of paper and wrote a note.

"In playing Hanging with Friends recently, I keep getting the same six letters every time, on either the top or bottom row. The letters are always KILLAL. Is this some sort of programming glitch? Can you upload a new version of the game to prevent this from happening? Thank you."

Alex signed his name to the e-mail, including his phone number.

Shortly afterwards, his cell phone actually rang, which was rare. (Alex mainly used his phone as a gaming device these days.)

"Hello?"

"Hi. This is Zynga headquarters. We just wanted you to know that we've uploaded the newest update of Hanging with Friends to your phone. That should solve the problem you've been having with the game." The voice was female and pleasant. Cheery, even.

"Thanks! It's not really much of a problem. It's just—weird. But thank you for fixing that. And one other thing, is there any way to communicate with a randomly chosen opponent? I'd like to congratulate WitchyWoman. She beats me quite frequently. She's really good." Alex chuckled aloud when he uttered that last line.

"Gee...I'm sorry, Mr. Bentley. It's all done with algorithms and hocus pocus. I'm sure the name must have come from your Facebook friends. Maybe you can look them over and figure it out? I can't help you. I don't think anyone here really knows the identities of the randomly chosen opponents—other than that they're people who are willing to play anyone, that is. That's the way it is now, anyway."

"Okay. Thanks, anyway."

Alex switched his phone off for the night. He plugged it in to power it up again. It was his custom to play first thing in the morning and last thing at night. It wasn't unusual for him to have twenty games going at once, not counting the Words with Friends Scrabble-like game, which he usually lost to Megan526. He played that one, too, but not as incessantly.

And never as successfully.

The next morning, Alex grabbed his Android phone and turned it on. It took forever to power up. While it did, the red glowing screen always reminded Alex of the "Tron" movie sequel. The futuristic cars. That sequel had been a bomb, but the cars were so creative! *It's a wonder they didn't get more Oscar nods*, Alex mused.

Alex pushed the button of the black-haired boy's face representing Words with Friends and Hanging with Friends. The game appeared.

WitchyWoman had left him a word to solve. It was a hard one. Alex had figured out this much: _ U _AT. He didn't have very many guesses left, and he had no idea what the word was. He decided to select "R" and—wonder of wonders—the middle letter *was* "R." Now, he had _ URAT. Alex still was clueless. He went through his old dictionary. No help. He turned on his computer and began inserting every letter in the alphabet, beginning with "B" (He already knew the word contained an "A"). When he hit "J", the online dictionary pronounced it to be a word. Something legal. Eureka! Alex keyed in a "J." Watched the spinning circle send the move. Celebrated when his guess was correct.

Take that, Witchy!

Now it was time for Alex to make a word for WitchyWoman. He pushed the buttons to get his twelve letters.

KILLAL

YRFUOC

FURIOUS. I can make FURIOUS. Oh, wait. I don't have an 'S.' Or another 'U.'

Alex settled for FURY and sent the word. The scrap of paper with the Zynga information on it was still cluttering his desk. Alex dialed the phone number for Zynga headquarters.

"Good afternoon, A&E Enterprises," the friendly female voice on the other end answered. Businesslike. Mechanical. *Strange that it's a real person answering in this day and age,* Alex thought. *But nice.* "A&E Enterprises? I thought this was Zynga headquarters," Alex said.

"Yes, Sir. It is. Or, rather, it was. Zynga was our predecessor. A&E bought Zynga two months ago. We're not changing the brand name, though. Too well known."

"What is *your* name, if you don't mind my asking?" Alex asked.

"I'm Ruth. How may I help you?"

"Well, Ruth, first of all, can you tell me what A&E stands for?"

"Sure. A&E is the abbreviation for 'Advise and Execute,' our parent company. We recently acquired several other companies. Zynga is one of them."

"Okay. I called Zynga about a week ago. My Hanging with Friends game is acting up. It keeps giving me the same letters, over and over. Sometimes the letters are the top line of the twelve. Sometimes the bottom. Always the same six letters. It's getting hard to make new words that fool my opponent when 50% of my letters are identical for each game. Can you help?"

"Sure. I can send you the new update," said Ruth.

"How new is the update?" asked Alex.

"It's been out for about two months. Should I send it now?"

"That's not going to do me any good. I was sent an update three days ago. My phone is still showing me the same letters on one line, over and over and over. To make matters worse, the six letters actually spell something." Alex waited for Ruth to ask what the letters spelled, but she seemed most interested in concluding the call.

"I'm sorry, Sir. I just answer phones and pass on messages. I could let the game designers know that you're having this problem. Maybe it's a flaw in the coding...something computer-related? I was an English major. I don't know anything about programming. I wouldn't be able to speculate on why you keep getting the same six letters. I'm sorry to hear that the upload didn't help. Perhaps you should try another upload?" Ruth sounded genuinely sorry to learn that Alex was having difficulty. She also sounded powerless to solve his problem.

Alex sighed. "No. That's okay. I'm probably playing this game entirely too much, anyway. I think I'll switch to Words with Friends for a while. Thanks, Ruth!"

Alex pushed the red button on his cell phone, ending the call and congratulated himself on how pleasant the call had been. *In the old days, I'd have bitten her head off! Before the P.G. era: pre-Geifman.*

He went back to his game, but, this time, he pushed the yellow "W" to bring up Words with Friends. Alex was not very good at Words with Friends. He lost almost every game. When he discussed his never-ending losses with one of his opponents (the friend with whom he played racquetball), Randy said, "Oh? Is the Big Man whining?" His racquetball opponent, Randy Washington, was as competitive as Alex. Randy had been beaten repeatedly at Hanging with Friends by Alex. He was happy to hear that Alex was not invincible.

"No, Randy. I'm not whining. I'm just explaining that, while *you* always get a 'Q' with a 'U,' I only get a 'Q' by itself. Unusable. All my other letters are usually worth one point. Two points max. It's hard to beat anyone at this game if all I have to work with are one-pointers. And, lately, at Hanging with Friends, I've been getting mainly 'L's,' which are only 2 points, so it's like a virus that's spreading. It's evil."

"Ooooo, poor baby. I feel SO sorry for you."

Randy actually did not feel sorry at all. Alex had beaten him without mercy in over 100 games of Hanging with Friends. It had not been pretty. Randy was secretly glad to see Alex humbled—finally.

Although self-employed, Alex traveled for his job. He did sales for his company's product, a self-propelled robotic vacuum cleaner. Sometimes, Alex did trade shows. Sometimes, he tried to swing a deal with a hotel chain to use them in their Hiltons or Holiday Inns. Alex could be very persuasive. But he could also lose his temper completely, if thwarted.

Alex was sitting in the First Class section of a Boeing 747 bound for Atlanta. Earlier, he had been worried that he wouldn't make it to O'Hare in time. The morning rush hour had been worse than usual. Fortunately, Alex always alotted extra time for just such emergencies. This morning had been no different. The cab driver had to get gas before heading out to the airport. Demonstrating his anger management progress, this had not upset Alex. (He kept repeating, to himself, *We have time. We have time.*) They pulled into the BP station where gas was the highest in a five-state region (Roosevelt and Wabash, near his condo building in the Central Station District). Alex didn't lash out verbally at the driver. (*Dr. Geifman would be proud of me.*) Although he could have. Maybe he should have. *But my shrink says I have to cut people some slack. I have to lighten up.... give people some leeway. Not raise my blood pressure. Take life easier. Let it flow. Breathe deeply. Count.*

Plus, Alex always allowed extra time for just such fuck-ups since entering treatment. That was why he found himself with so much extra time to kill in the airport.

Alex waited in the chairs near the boarding gate for a long time. He was able to begin ten new games of Words with Friends during that time. Nobody responded immediately.

However, Alex noticed that WitchyWoman had responded to his last Hanging with Friends word: "*Watch WitchyWoman's solve attempt*" the phone said. The infernal machine seemed to be demanding it, in fact.

Unh huh, thought Alex. *Not gonna' do it.*

Alex had ten responses from three players for Hanging with Friends, but he was pretty sure he would be fucked on the "make up a word for your opponent" front. Every time—or every other time—Alex would get KILLAL. It was getting harder and harder to make words that WitchyWoman, in particular, didn't guess almost immediately. And the letters, except for the K, were worth very little. So Alex doggedly stuck to his plan of moving to the new Words with Friends Scrabble-like game.

Nobody was responding to Words with Friends. He was fidgety and bored. Alex was only able to make the word CAN. It was the only word he had. Not many points. No double words. No double letters. Nada. Zip. Zero.

Even Zyrgfwat will beat me every single game of Words with Friends if this keeps up, Alex thought to himself. Disconsolate. He fidgeted with the arm rest and wished he hadn't just given up smoking. The plane boarded. Alex was near the front. He got out his Android.

I suck at this game. Maybe I'll just try Hanging with Friends one last time. I'll solve the words that Witchy and friends have already sent me. Sort of tidy up.

The steward was coming down the aisle. He stopped by Alex's seat just as Alex began solving what would turn out to be VICTIM.

"I'm thorry, Thir. You'll have to turn off your phone now. All electronic gameth and inthtrumenth—computerth, Ipodth, Ipadth mutht be turned off before take-off."

"Right," Alex said, barely glancing at the steward who was standing over him. "I'm almost done."

"Thir. You're done NOW! You have to turn off your phone. NOW! It'th federal law."

The steward, who looked like a younger version of Wally Cox, was forcing the issue. He had a distinct lisp. He stood about five feet six inches.

His peeved tone of voice did not reinforce the image of "friendly skies." (Or, in the steward's case, "friendly thieth.")

"Yeth, I hear you, Thir," said Alex, mimicking the effeminate steward. He felt himself slipping into *I'm pissed* mode. Alex hadn't visited that neighborhood for a while. He missed it. It felt as though someone had just held a ribbon-cutting in his brain. The ribbon that had been cut was Alex's self control.

The steward grabbed for Alex's phone. At the same moment, anticipating the small man's move, Alex pulled it away from the steward's grasp. Alex felt a surge of alpha male testosterone welling up from deep within, anger that he had been suppressing for many months. Dr. Geifman's admonitions were gone from Alex's consciousness.

This is MY phone. Who do you think you are, you little pissant?

The man reminded Alex of his least favorite teacher of all time, Mr. Clark. Mr. Clark, his history teacher, had been a bully. He belittled students in his classes with impunity.

Alex had not yet fastened his seatbelt. He stood up. He was on the aisle. The two men were a mismatch in size, Alex standing nearly a foot taller than the short steward. The red-faced steward was angry. Alex was also angry. (*Angry, angrier, angriest—or should it be angry, more angry, most angry?*) Alex's deep-seated anger had been suppressed ever since the DUI a year ago; it had been building ever since.

This isn't fair! he screamed inwardly.

A wrestling match over Alex's android phone ensued.

The two men fell to the floor, struggling awkwardly. As the steward went down, his head hit the sharp edge of the cart he had been pushing to the front area, preparatory to loading it with soft drinks and coffee and pay-through-the-nose-for-it snacks. Blood. Thuds. Screams from women passengers seated nearby. The steward's head made a horrible noise. The sound of a baseball bat hitting a melon. He lay still. Alex, no longer clutching his phone, which was in the aisle, towered over the tiny man, breathing heavily.

Two male passengers nearby jumped Alex at the same time. They wrestled him to the floor. One very large man sat on him, holding him for the authorities. A female stewardess phoned breathlessly, asking for help from the ground crew. She sounded semi-hysterical.

"Quick! Somebody! We've got a fight in the first row. Man down! Get a doctor. Allan's hurt."

"We'll be there in five," a voice on the other end of the phone responded.

Alex lay there on the floor, immobilized. His phone had fallen from his grasp. It was in the aisle near him. He could see the twelve letters laid out on the phone's screen for him to form the word for WitchyWoman. The top line said **KILLAL.**

Alex had stopped struggling after the third large passenger piled on. It was inevitable. He must wait for the authorities and plead his case.

After all, we weren't even close to being airborne when the steward insisted I turn off my phone. We hadn't even pulled away from the gate! Does turning a cell phone on or off on an airplane really do anything? Alex doubted it. He'd be exonerated. He was surprised that the mousy steward (*Mr. Clark, in Alex's mind*) hadn't stirred.

With the three male passengers holding him down, his struggles subsiding, Alex strained his neck to see the steward. Other passengers were using their cell phones to record video of Alex and friends that would turn up on Youtube and the six o'clock news.

The guy's just lying there. I hope he isn't really hurt.

Alarm bells were beginning to sound in Alex's head. The steward wasn't moving. At all. He was as still as the air in the ominous seconds before a tornado strikes. He wasn't moaning. Glassy-eyed. Blood gushing from a large gash near his left temple.

Oh, shit!

Alex was just barely able to breathe. One of the passengers had Alex's neck in a choke-hold (*soon to be declared illegal in New Jersey after an unfortunate strangulation death.*) Alex was really struggling to breathe.

Alex saw one more thing before he blacked out: the steward's name tag.

It read, in big bold letters over the airline's logo:

Hi! I'm Al!

Circle Eight:
The Fraudulent

The Mirror

"The mirror should tell us something," Sheriff Joe Bates said to Deputy Brad Norton.

"What do you mean?" Brad asked. The Deputy was puzzled.

"I mean that there's wreckage…actual pieces of the car that hit poor old Tom are down there in the ditch with him." The Sheriff indicated the corpse in the ditch below them with a nod of his head.

Joe hitched up his uniform pants. He adjusted himself. The male gesture so many of his colleagues on the force imitated to show their virility. Brad sniffled in the wind and freezing cold, wondering if he should climb down into the ditch or stay where he was.

"We ought to be able to get a fix on the make and model of the vehicle, anyway, from the debris." Joe gestured with a nod of his head towards the broken glass and shattered pieces of mirror lying all around the body, on the roadway and in the ditch itself. There were also twisted wires lying next to the corpse in the shallow ditch. A sign, said Sheriff Bates, that the side mirror was the kind that could be heated.

"That mirror came from an expensive vehicle," he said, stating the obvious. "Only the more expensive, newer ones offer heated mirrors."

"Why would anyone want a heated mirror?" Brad asked, perplexed.

"Nevermind about that. The point is, we might be able to get a lead on the hit-and-run that killed poor Tom Thomas from narrowing down the vehicles that have heated mirrors and were sold in Muscatine County. Find those that are registered around these parts."

Brad didn't say it, but he thought, to himself, *Sounds like a lot of work for somebody. And I'll just bet it's not going to be you, Joe.*

What Brad did say, aloud, was, "Right. I'll get Wally and the evidence technicians out here to bag everything." He shifted his weight uneasily in the bitter biting wind that chilled them both deep to the bone as they stood on the slanted slushy hillside a mile out of town.

"Hell! Get the coroner out here ASAP to bag poor Tom. He's layin' there half naked, frozen nearly solid. He's been layin' there for 3 months. Let's get his body into the morgue," said Sheriff Joe. Joe sniffed and spat. Another male affectation.

It was cold. Damn cold. Yes, it was March, but it had been one hell of a winter, and the forecast was for more snow tomorrow. It was the coldest March in fifty-four years, and the thirteenth coldest since 1871 when records started being kept. The average temperature this month was only twenty-nine degrees—well below freezing. And the first day of spring was past. Only six of the past month's temperatures in March had been *above* normal.

Before that, there had been snow. Lots and lots of snow. So far this winter there had been nearly eighty-seven inches of snow—well above the normal thirty-six inches they usually got in Atalissa, Iowa.

Since October fifteenth, the temperature had been below freezing for sixty-nine straight days. Twenty-three of those days, the temperature was well below zero. Fifty percent of this rural area in southwest Iowa was still covered with snow, to an average depth of six inches. In January when Tom had actually disappeared, there were several feet of the white stuff everywhere and it had been coming down like snow in a shaken snow globe the night Tom vanished.

It was no wonder they couldn't find him that night. Sheriff Joe Bates looked at Tom Thomas' half-naked cadaver and shivered.

Henry's Turkey Farm had been a fixture in the small Iowa town of Atalissa for so long that most of the 271 (*and two old grouches, as the town's welcome sign said*) inhabitants of Atalissa knew the twenty-five boys and men by name.

The boys and men came from Goldthwaite, Texas to work killing turkeys. After they killed them, they prepared them for sale in West Liberty, Iowa. They killed the birds and then ripped the innards from the poultry. Some days, "the boys," as they were known, killed and gutted 27,000 or

28,000 turkeys—all by hand. They worked from five in the morning till dark.

And, under Vern Clark, when they weren't actively working, Vern expected the Atalissa crew to continue exercising in the gym, so as to become stronger so that the boys could toil even harder and longer killing and preparing turkeys for the plant in West Liberty, Iowa—a town that boasted its fame as the birthplace of the only Iowa president ever elected, Herbert Hoover.

One of the men, Willie Johnson, told Joe and Brad during the investigation, "It got real bad after Mr. Henry left and Mr. Clark took over. Vern called us names. Called me stupid. Kicked us. Once, he called me a stupid black bastard and handcuffed me to my bed. The night he disappeared, Tom was told to stand holding a heavy waste can above his head for a long time—hours—because he wouldn't go to bed when Vern told him to."

Willie's brown eyes watered. and the black skin of his face creased in a look that made it appear he might break into tears at any moment. Willie continued, "Tom said he was going to watch TV like everybody else. He said it real loud. Vern told him, 'If you don't want to do like you're told, there's the door.' Tom walked through it. At the time, he wasn't wearin' nothin' but his pajama bottoms. He was too mad to dress right to go outside. I mean for the cold that night. We never saw Tom alive again."

Willie wiped his sixty-something eyes with the back of his hand and glanced away. Brad pretended to be taking notes, to give the man his privacy. Sheriff Joe looked away, as though he hadn't noticed the elderly man's unseemly display of emotion.

At the outset of the experiment in giving jobs to the mentally defective, Kenneth Henry assured the townsfolk (*and the men themselves*) that the place they were going to in Iowa was better than the west Texas town of Goldthwaite that they came from. That wasn't hard for the men to believe. In Texas, they lived within the system. They were housed in institutions for the developmentally disabled called state schools. Mostly, they were warehoused with little or nothing to do.

Each man was promised a good job in Iowa and a retirement community back in Goldthwaite when their workdays were over. Since each man was of limited intelligence (*and all had had trouble finding work*), the promises made convinced them to sign on and make the move. Trusting. Naive. Most had just the I.Q. of a child. They all would later be classified as trainable mentally handicapped or worse by the social service agency of the state of Iowa.

The ten men—(*one who was eleven years old was really only a child, himself*)— traveled by bus to Atalissa in Muscatine County. They took up residence in a big green building on a hillside just outside of town almost twenty years before, just as the Bracero program was being phased out in the sixties. That program had allowed canny operators to bring Mexican immigrants into the country to harvest crops. After that program ended in the sixties, the boys arrived soon after—another group ripe for the hustle. Another bunch of unfortunates to take advantage of, if you were smart and played your cards right.

The garish green building with the eight windows on one side, the dormitory for the boys, had been a schoolhouse. It was refurbished slightly for the twenty men from Texas. It wasn't much to look at from the outside, standing up on the hillside outside of town. Standing silently apart, like a giant green thumb. Its own little water tower nearby. The green paint was too bright. It was Mexican bright. The lawn was well tended, at first. Still, the garish green of the former schoolhouse didn't blend harmoniously with the natural green of the grass on the hill.

For a while, it looked and felt like home to the men. That was before Vern Clark started chaining the doors from the outside. Vern started chaining them after Tom Thomas walked out to protest the treatment he was receiving and to assert his right to watch TV like all the other men.

"But," said Kenneth Henry, as he helped the men from the small bus that first day (often called "the short bus"), ushering them into the bilious green building, "It's real nice inside. You boys will be well taken care of. That's a promise. We got a gym for you…a pool table. You'll like it here."

And then Kenneth Henry left and drove back to Texas, leaving a local couple in charge, Dolores and Vern Clark.

For a while, the men did like it in Atalissa.

They traveled into town with their money and spent it at the Atalissa Mini-Mart. They showed up at the 9:30 a.m. Sunday school services at the local Methodist Church. Although they had trouble reciting the Lord's Prayer, they liked to sing, and they liked to dance. They dressed up as clowns for the Atalissa Fourth of July parade. They wore cloaks and headgear as the Wise Men and shepherds at Christmas for the church's pageant.

But all was not as it appeared.

Levi Willie, one of Tom Thomas' fellow workers, described a typical day. "I get up early, when the sun rises. Gotta' go to work early. I can make 'em come to me. (*Here Levi gobbled like a tom turkey, his own neck wattles jiggling*). The birds'd come right up to me. I'd get 'em. I'd pat them on the belly when I put them on the shackle. That settles 'em down. 'Calm down, Tom,' I'd tell 'em. And they would— until it was too late." Levi laughed like a small child, gleefully, recalling his skill with the birds.

Billy Penter chimed in, "The turkeys'd hang in the middle of the shackles. The shackles'd move down the row. We have to kill 'em. Too damn bloody. One day we kilt 27,000 birds. Next day, we come back and did 28,000. My job is to stick my hand in and pull their guts out." Billy shook his head slowly from side to side "It ruins your fingers. I had to go to the emergency room five times to have my wrists drained."

Here, Billy held up his scarred wrists in silent testimony to the hours of backbreaking labor, stretching over a quarter century. Billy was scheduled for carpal tunnel syndrome surgery, if the money from the lawsuit ever came through—the money the boys won in court after everything went to Hell. Two hundred and forty million dollars, in all. Fifty thousand dollars per man. But there was no money. Henry's Turkey Farm went belly-up. As Brad Norton said to Sheriff Bates, "You can't get blood out of a turnip, Boss." It was an old saying, but it fit.

When Sheriff Joe went to the bunkhouse to speak with the men, he discovered that now—three months after Tom's disappearance—there were chains on the outside of the building's doors. Vern Clark wasn't taking any chances that his entire crew would walk off.

The chains came about because Tom had accepted Vern's dare and—although he had no coat and no shoes, (and was clad only in pajama bottoms at the time)—he left in January. If Tom had been a smarter man, he would have grabbed his coat. Put on his shoes. Taken some money. But none of the boys in the bunkhouse were smart.

For months, no one knew where Tom Thomas was. Vern went after him immediately, driving his Honda CR-VS. Vern had left the room after throwing down the gauntlet. He knew that nobody sane would go outside in this weather, clad only in pajama bottoms, wearing no shoes and no coat, while a blizzard was in progress.

Vern hadn't thought that through. The boys weren't capable of thinking tactically. Therefore, they were taken advantage of, time and time again. There are some things worse than death, if a man gets put down enough.

As soon as Vern re-entered the bunkhouse and learned that Tom had actually gone out into that night's frigid blizzard, he alerted the law. Sheriff Bates and his men arrived and police combed the area. The snow was so deep that Tom's half-clothed body wasn't found until March, after the thaw set in. Piles of snow in the ditches of Highway 61 and Highway 6 began to melt. Animals that fell into the deep ravine next to the gravel road were now becoming visible in the spring thaw.

Before that, back at the bright green schoolhouse dormitory, Vern and Dolores Clark ruled the boys with an iron boot.

The stories the boys told were horrifying.

For all their hard work, they were paid only $65.71 in take home cash monthly—roughly 44 cents an hour. It was less than prison inmates at the Fort Madison Penitentiary. Living conditions were worse than incarceration. After ten years of no upkeep, the insulation in the old schoolhouse began to fall from the ceilings. Asbestos. Rats. Bugs. Cold. The building was not fit for human habitation, yet twenty-five men lived there for twenty-five years, laboring long, hard, and bloodily every day. Abused. Degraded. Called names. Handcuffed. Kicked if they didn't rise quickly enough to work 12-hour shifts.

"Get your black butt in that gym and lift those weights," Vern said to Billy, kicking Billy with his booted toe.

When Tom Thomas bolted for freedom, Vern Clark knew he couldn't allow that. He panicked. Vern quickly followed in his Honda CR-VS, searching for Tom—a brand-new vehicle bought with money saved from the men's earnings. Seven hundred and fifty dollars per man was deducted each month to pay for their miserable living conditions, their food and their clothing. That left only $65.71 spending money for each man. All this was neatly recorded in a ledger entitled *The Magic of Simplicity*, an ironic title.

Tom's Honda van cost $17,000. It took twenty-two months of just one of the boy's wages in the ledger to pay for Vern's car. Vern's wife, Dolores, drove a new Honda Pilot EXLs van. Even fancier, it cost $24,000.

It was snowing outside—another of the winter's interminable blizzards. Vern told Sheriff Bates that Tom just wandered off. He didn't give the Sheriff the real details of Tom's departure. At the time, the men immediately began looking over the surrounding terrain for signs of footprints in the deep snow. Something that might lead them to the runaway.

When Sheriff Joe checked Vern Clark's van, there was no sign of any kind of collision. The side mirrors on both the driver and passenger sides were the original mirrors. Dolores was gone that day. She was taking care of her mother at Lantern Park Nursing Home in Iowa City.

The search for the car with the missing mirror continued. Beyond knowing it was a Honda with a mirror that was capable of heating up, there wasn't much the authorities discovered. Vern Clark's van and side mirror was undamaged.

Dolores Clark spent three days by her mother's bedside. Influenza was sweeping the nursing home. The staff wasn't sure that Dolores' elderly mother would make it. But she did.

While Dolores' elderly mother—Vern Clark's mother-in-law—was fighting for her life, Dolores had a few small repairs done to *her* van. Her brother Bobby worked at a body shop in Coralville. Bobby had an impressive array of tools in his own garage at home. The bachelor was a gearhead who liked to tinker with cars. He had made it his life's work.

"Bobby, I want you to fix this here side mirror in your garage. Don't tell a soul."

"Why not?" Bobby asked his sister. He sounded puzzled.

"What you don't know won't hurt you. Just fix it. Say nothing about it to anyone," Dolores replied.

Bobby did as he was asked. He assumed it had something to do with not reporting the damage so that Dolores' insurance rates wouldn't go up. That was always the risk in reporting accidents to insurance companies.

When Bobby asked her how her mirror got smashed, Dolores said, "A deer came staggering up outta' the ditch there on I-380, on my way to Cedar Rapids. Stumbled right into the side of my car. I'm just lucky I wasn't killed. I sped up as fast as I could when I saw him comin' at me out of the corner of my eye. Saw him in my peripheral vision. Heard the dumb thing hit the mirror. I was afraid to slow down, for fear he'd run right in front of the van. So, I just tried to outrun him. Guess I was lucky, huh? He just hit the mirror and bounced off. Probably died in the ditch."

"Yeah. Probably," agreed Bobby. "You sure were lucky. If he had gotten in front of your car, the damage to your brand new fancy Honda Pilot would be a whole lot worse. Could have taken out your whole front grill. You might have lost control. On the good news front, I can fix it as good as new. Nobody'll ever be the wiser."

Bobby winked at his older sister. He smiled. He thought she was trying to keep the mirror repair a secret from her husband Vern. Vern had a nasty disposition and a bad temper. Everybody in Muscatine County knew it. Bobby understood why Dolores would want her van fixed with no fuss and no comment to her surly husband.

Dolores smiled back. Bobby made it as good as new with some parts from a used car the same make and model. Everything was working out real good. Nobody would ever know.

"Who'll miss one more deer, anyway?" Bobby said to his sister, as he used a wrench to tighten a bolt. "They're like vermin. They ain't no good to anybody and they're thick as weeds. We oughta' be able to just take a gun to them, like they do in Scott County out at Davenport's Scott County Park. I'm just glad you weren't hurt, Sis, and that your Pilot wasn't banged up worse."

"Oh, I know, Bobby. I know," said Dolores, nodding her head in agreement. "And I think you're right. We *should* be allowed to take guns to 'em. Damn pests. Nobody will miss one more when there are so many around just causing trouble and not doing any good for anybody. Maybe next time they shoot 'em in Scott County Park I'll go up there and see if I can shoot me one or two." Dolores smiled at Bobby. They both laughed.

Dolores buttoned her coat against the chill and prepared to leave. She smirked again as she pulled into the gravel driveway leading to the house she and Vern shared.

O

Circle Nine:
The Treacherous

A Losing Hand

The twitter read: "Bloody knuckles—Guess I was in a fight. #backdown." Kiran Govindiah wiped his injured knuckles with a washcloth hanging in the bathroom. He was at a house party in a rural unincorporated area near Southern Illinois University (Carbondale, Illinois).

It was February 12, 2014, a Wednesday night. The Midwest was in the grip of a Polar vortex with temperatures plummeting to thirty below zero.

Kiran won $1,000 playing Texas Hold 'Em. The six boys played for hours. One of the other players—his roommate, cousin and best friend, Pravin Govindiah—lost big.

Normally, Pravin was easy-going, like Kiran, but Pravin had been drinking. When Kiran announced he was going back to the dorm to study for his Physics test in the morning, Pravin balked. He demanded that Kiran stay. Offer them all an opportunity to win their money back.

"Come on, Kiran! Be a sport! Don't be a sore winner. Let us have a shot at winning back some of our money," Pravin said. Initially, Pravin sounded reasonable. He was slurring his words, but, seemed okay otherwise. As time went by and Kiran did not relent, Pravin began to turn resentful.

Alone in the kitchen, still facing Kiran's resistance to continuing the game, Privan actually took a swing at his cousin when Kiran mocked Privan's card-playing ability. Kiran was a well-known jokester. He meant no harm by his remarks. But Privan was pretty well lubricated by that time. Besides, he was the big loser in the game.

"Just stay and play a few more hands," Privan pleaded. Wheedling. The booze talking.

"Naaah, man. I gotta' get back and study for my Physics exam in the morning." Kiran playfully punched his roommate, Pravin, in the shoulder adding, "Hey, Pravin—don't give up your day job any time soon. No delusions about becoming a professional gambler, I hope." Kiran smiled his super-wide Obama-style wide white-toothed smile.

Pravin failed to see the humor in the remark. He swung wildly at his cousin and roommate.

Teasing was Kiran's stock in trade. He joked around with everybody. He hadn't expected his cousin to react with violence. Kiran instinctively put his hands up in a defensive posture. The beer can still clutched in Privan's fist did a number on the Master Gambler's knuckles. [*Hence, Kiran's twitter post.*]

Kiran backed away from his cousin. "Hey! I'm a lover, not a fighter. I just like to play cards. Chill, man!" Kiran, the card game's big winner realized he'd have to find a different ride home. The two had come together in Privan's car.

All night long, Kiran nursed his beer and won. He won a lot. When asked if he wanted another drink, Kiran said, "No thanks, Bro'. I'm still good." He would hold up the beer can that had been his companion for the entire evening. He remained uncannily lucky at poker, while Privan continued to consistently lose. Kiran *was* the best player in his SIU (Southern Illinois University) dorm.

After dorm games, Kiran would say, "Hey, Buddy! I'm lucky. What can I tell you? I'm going to kick over the traces. Head west. Go west young man! Get away from these brutal winters." Kiran said the last line and then pretended to shiver from the cold.

Pravin would bring him back to Earth, saying, "Yes, I can just see your parents *really* going for that."

It was an inside joke. Kiran's mom and dad and his older sister Lovely were completely integral to his life. They were a close-knit family. That was why Kiran expressed his opinion that Matt Slade was not a good match for his older sister, Lovely, when the two began dating. Mainly, he teased Lovely, but his barely-concealed disapproval stung.

His entire family supported Kiran wholeheartedly. He wanted to become a physicist. His mathematical prowess was well-documented. He had graduated from the Illinois Math and Science Academy with Honors. His family would not encourage or tolerate a career for Kiran as a professional gambler. Each family member had a lot of power to veto wrong moves by any of the others. Realistically, Kiran, himself, didn't want to play cards for a living.

But Kiran liked to win. It was fun earning extra cash in friendly games with his college buddies.

Only a few in the group groused about their losses that night as long or as loudly as Privan. That made Privan a prime suspect when Kiran went missing.

"Yeah. I was upset. Kiran was way better than me at cards. And everything else, for that matter." Privan sniffled, still suffering from the cold he had picked up during the search for Kiran outdoors in the woods. Still, Privan denied responsibility for his best friend and cousin's death.

"In fact," Officer Matthew Slade said, "didn't you take a swing at Kiran?" Matt waited for a response.

"Well—yeah—after Kiran won all night long and was up by a grand, he wanted to quit and go home." Privan looked miffed. "We rode together. I drove. I wanted a chance to win some of my money back. That's all."

"How much did you lose?" Slade asked.

Privan shuffled his feet. He sniffled again. "I dunno'. I know Kiran won a lot."

"Isn't it true, Privan, that you lost at least $500 of the $1,000 that Kiran won?"

Matthew knew the figure because the other players confirmed it. Kiran won at least a cool grand that night from the six involved in the game. Matt also knew because Kiran's older sister (Lovely) told him so. Lovely and Kiran told each other everything. They were as close as a brother and a sister can be. At least, they were until she began dating Matt Slade.

Lovely was upset that Kiran disapproved of Matt, but she downplayed the seriousness of their romance. The truth was that she and Matt had been talking marriage. She knew her parents would want her to find a nice Indian boy. She could just imagine Kiran's reaction if she and Matt were to become engaged.

Lovely called Matt the night he disappeared.

"Hey, Matt. Can you swing by the party my brother's at? He's stranded there without a ride. Something about winning at cards. His cousin Pravin is mad at him, and Pravin was his ride. Maybe you could give him a lift home? He shouldn't be walking in this cold. Besides, Kiran left me a voicemail that says he won over $1,000. It's not safe to be hitchhiking in this kind of weather, let alone with that kind of cash."

Matt agreed to do Lovely the favor, even though he knew Kiran disapproved of him.

Matt had met the beautiful Indian girl at a Support Your Community function six months earlier where he was the speaker. Lovely was seriously beautiful. Matt asked Lovely out. He joked, at the time, "You are aptly named."

The two came from very different backgrounds. Matt wanted more from Lovely than she wanted from him, at first. Over time, they each became more serious about the relationship. However, they downplayed it to the world.

The cop waited for Privan's answer to his question. "Well, yeah—I *might* have lost that much," Privan said, tentatively. "My folks had just sent me a check to pay for some stuff. I cashed it right before the party. I wasn't planning on betting at all that night. I still had it on me. It just—happened."

Privan looked uncomfortable. Remorseful. "And, yes, I did take a swing at Kiran after he refused to stay and play. He wouldn't let any of us have a chance to win our money back. But I was drunk."

"Was Kiran drunk?"

"Naaah. That was part of Kiran's strategy. He'd get a beer and nurse it. He'd pretend to be drinking all night. But he never really drank. Ever."

Officer Slade knew this, too.

The autopsy reports showed no drugs or alcohol in the victim's body. The official verdict: Kiran Govindiah froze to death from exposure. Hypothermia.

Now, it was up to Matthew Slade and other officers to determine how a religious 19-year-old honors student who called home every day, didn't drink, and had no criminal record ended up dead in a field three miles from a party.

His mother, recounting how the police broke the news of Kiran's disappearance said, "My heart just stopped." News Channel Nine snippet recorded her tearfully saying, "Once they start college and are out of sight, you can't protect them. Kiran called every day. He never talked back—even when he was a little boy. He couldn't be mad at anyone for long. I don't understand how this could have happened."

She broke down in tears at that point and her husband led her away. The talking head reporter moved on to a story about the teachers' union strike.

When Kiran didn't show up for his physics test the next day, Thursday, February 13th, he was reported missing. It would be six days before his frozen body was found.

It was five days before Officer Matt Slade turned in a report of an encounter with a parked pick-up truck—an old battered green Ford—parked on the shoulder of the highway, hazard lights blinking, near the party location. Matt said he stopped and asked the driver if he could help.

When questioned later, Matt said, "Well, this truck driver—white guy, about 6' 3"—was standing outside his truck. He was by himself. He told me he was on his way home when he saw a black guy walking east along the highway. The truck driver told me, 'I offered to give him a ride, but I told him I'd need money for gas—especially since the black guy kept changing his mind about where he wanted to go. At that point—when I told him I wanted money for gas—he hit me. Then he ran into the woods.'"

In the report, Matt added the detail that there was a red contusion on the trucker's cheek. "The truck driver said he chased the man, but he couldn't find him."

Department superiors asked Matt, "Did you search for the black man at that time?"

"Yes, Sir. I followed departmental protocol. I scanned the area with my flashlight. I didn't see anything. Remember, the trucker said it was a *black* guy. Kiran is Indian, not black. It never occurred to me that the truck driver was talking about Kiran Govindiah."

"Is that why you didn't file a report about this mysterious truck driver until six days had passed?" The Internal Affairs Investigator found this point particularly odd.

Matt's response: "I was dealing with some personal stuff at the time. I was helping look for Kiran on the ground. I was tromping around with a lot of volunteers for six days. I just never made the connection between the truck driver who mentioned a *BLACK* guy hitchhiking and Kiran. Everyone who knew Kiran knows he would never hit a stranger in the face for no good reason. Kiran was someone who could never hold a grudge. He had a big heart. I can't imagine that he'd just hit the truck driver like that. Ask anyone who knew him. Of course," added Matt, planting the seed " maybe the truck driver *did* strike Kiran or attacked him in some way. I knew Kiran. I was looking for him, to give him a ride home. His sister called me and said he needed a ride. But the only person I found was the truck driver."

The Bureau of Internal Affairs Investigator interrogating Matthew Slade repositioned himself in the chair opposite the rookie officer. "You knew the Govindiah family—is that correct?"

"Well, I really only know Kiran's older sister, Lovely."

"And you say that Kiran's older sister contacted you and requested that you drive out to the party location and look for her younger brother that night? Was that normal police procedure: giving a hitchhiker a ride home because his sister asked you to?"

Matt looked momentarily befuddled. "Lovely and I—we'd had a few dates. I was doing her a favor. She was a friend."

"A good friend?"

"Yes, a good friend. But my search was concentrated farther from the party location. I looked where we thought Kiran would be. He started walking ninety minutes before the voicemail he left. Lovely and I thought that Kiran would be at least ten miles from the party by then. He left a message that said he had won at cards, that he was walking home. Kiran was a track star at Niles Township High School before he went to the Illinois Math and Science Academy, you know. It didn't make any sense that he'd be in the location the truck driver described. Plus, Kiran wasn't black."

"Why didn't you get the name and address of the truck driver?"

"I actually did get a name and address—James White—but it turned out to be false."

"You didn't ask for identification?"

"Guy said he'd forgotten his wallet, which is why he asked for money for gas."

"Did you write him up?"

"No, Sir."

"Does that seem like good police work, to you?"

"No, sir."

"Would you do things differently, if given the chance to do them over?"

"Well, yes—obviously, I would. If I thought that that truck driver had anything to do with hurting Kiran—well, let's just say that I screwed up when I didn't demand identification more forcefully or give him a ticket when he couldn't provide it. I was preoccupied with his story of a black guy who ran into the woods. We both began searching immediately. If I had known then what I know now…." Matt's voice trailed off.

"Where, exactly, was Kiran's body found?" the Investigator asked.

"Three miles from the party. In a wooded area. Face down. It was very rough terrain. An extremely muddy trail. In the dark, it would have been slippery. Almost impossible to walk through there. There would have been no logical reason to run into that field, unless Kiran had some sort of fight with the guy in the truck. Or a fight with someone else. Kiran would stick to the main road. That's where I was looking for him. I began looking about five miles away from the site of the party. On his phone message to his sister, Kiran mentioned seeing lights in the distance. He said it looked like it might be a convenience store parking lot. There's a 7/11 further down the highway. Nothing at all in the area where I found the truck driver parked on the shoulder of the road."

The Bureau Investigator shuffled some papers. "Did you detain this truck driver at all? Maybe take him into the station to get a statement?"

"I took his statement, but I didn't realize, at the time, that he might be describing Kiran. As I noted earlier, I did not see any identification. He told me he left it at home."

Both men sat there in stony silence.

"Tell us what you know from talking to the boy's sister. You said her name was Lovely?"

"Yes, Sir." Matthew gathered his thoughts, preparing to recite his story.

"Around 12:30 a.m., about ninety minutes after he actually left the party, Kiran phoned Lovely. He left her a voicemail.

The investigator interrupted. "Lovely didn't actually speak directly with her brother, then?"

"No, Sir."

"Okay. Go on."

"Lovely said it sounded like Kiran had been running. He sounded out of breath. Upset. Kiran said Privan was angry with him. Since he went to the party in Privan's car, Kiran said he was walking home. He would try to hitch a ride into town."

I've told you this already, Matt thought to himself.

"When she called me to go give him a ride, Lovely told me that her parents would be really angry if they knew that Kiran was hitchhiking. Her exact words were, 'Mom and Dad would kill Kiran if they found out he was hitchhiking.'"

Unconscious irony. Matthew paused. "She sounded really upset. I just wanted to help her out, if I could." He continued, "She said their parents would also be really upset if they knew her brother was at a party where there was underage drinking. They didn't even like it that he gambled for fun. But Kiran wasn't drinking. He didn't do drugs. The family is upset that the press has made it sound as though Kiran was under the influence of alcohol or drugs and passed out in the woods after the party. That's not what happened."

"What did happen, Officer Slade? Do you know?" The investigator gave Matt a piercing look. Matt remained calm.

"No, Sir. Kiran was a good kid. He was always smiling. He always made other people laugh. He called home every day. He went to church.

He was at the party, yes, but he wasn't doing anything bad. He wasn't drunk. He wasn't doing drugs. He liked to tease people and make them laugh."

Lovely, Kiran's older sister—two years older at 21—was interviewed by the authorities. Lovely told the Internal Affairs Investigator of the phone message from Kiran. She told them about Kiran's Tweet about bruised knuckles and backing down from a fight.

Lovely said then, " I was so upset at that point that I called someone I knew—someone I've been dating—a local policeman. I knew he was working in the area that night. I asked him if he could take a ride past the location of the party. I thought maybe Matt could give Kiran a ride home. Kiran *was* hitchhiking. Hitchhiking is dangerous."

The irony of her words did not resonate with Lovely.

"That would be Matt Slade?" The Internal Affairs investigator asked.

"Yes," Lovely said. "We want answers. Until we find satisfying answers, we won't have peace of mind. We don't know who is safe any more. Our family is broken. Our priority is to find out what really happened. We just want answers. We aren't seeking revenge. We want answers."

Five Months Later:

The investigation dragged on from February until June. Kiran's parents demanded another autopsy be conducted. "The Chicago or St. Louis police departments would never conduct such a shoddy investigation," Kiran's mother said, defiantly, at the time. Distraught at her son's unexpected passing, and the way in which authorities apparently wanted to conceal the truth and brush facts and details under the rug, Mrs. Govindiah, a nurse, and her husband, a local businessman, employed a forensic pathologist suggested by Colonial Wojciechowski Funeral Home in Niles, the funeral home that handled Kiran's burial.

On June 3rd, the second forensic pathologist, Dr. James Carr, issued his report. It was in direct conflict with the official verdict of the police coroner: "The underlying cause of death for Kiran Govindiah was blunt force trauma to the head. Another person injured Kiran. There was a punch mark on the left side of his head. A defensive wound on his right arm. Those marks indicate he was trying to defend himself. There were many additional marks on the body *not* consistent with the original autopsy report that Kiran Govindiah died of hypothermia."

In a Channel 9 interview, Dr. Carr stated: "Kiran may have been alive for at least a day after he was injured. The defensive wound on his arm had started to heal. It's not clear whether the head injuries caused his death or whether they incapacitated him and led to hypothermia and it was the hypothermia which killed him."

At this point, the new autopsy pathologist went into remarks about "the underlying cause of death" and "the immediate cause of death." "For example, " Carr said, as the cameras turned, "A car accident might be the underlying cause of death because it gave a person a broken bone and he threw a blood clot that caused a stroke, with the embolism being the immediate cause of death. My mother died in a nursing home after influenza swept the facility. Her immediate cause of death was listed as pneumonia. But the influenza epidemic brought on her pneumonia. Her death certificate said pneumonia and old age. But influenza was what precipitated her death. Kiran died from blunt force trauma to his head. That was never even mentioned in the original autopsy. Whether those

blows knocked him out and he subsequently froze to death is open to question."

Dr. Carr gathered his papers and left the podium set up for his news conference.

Mrs. Govindiah, overcome with grief, was shown on camera saying, "It's really hard. We're not getting anywhere. We're facing more questions than answers. Why would the chief witness, the truck driver, simply be let go without a serious attempt to establish his true identity? Isn't getting a person's name and address the very first thing a policeman should do? This investigation was hopelessly botched. Officer Slade's encounter with the man in the truck was mishandled. He should have taken that man to head-quarters. Gotten his official statement. Officer Slade should have filed his report about the conversation much, much sooner. It took an entire week! In that week, my son died. Alone. Injured. In the woods. From the cold."

One of the reporters present at the news conference interjected, "But Officer Slade said that the truck driver told him he picked up a black man. Wasn't that why he didn't make the connection between the hitchhiker and Kiran?"

"I know what Officer Slade said, but he should have gotten the truck driver's testimony. And why did it take so long to even mention the stranded truck driver in the first place? This entire investigation has been one long attempt at pulling the wool over everyone's eyes. The police want the public to think Kiran was a bad kid who was drinking or doing drugs. They want us to believe it was an accident that he froze to death. The police released an autopsy that never mentioned Kiran's defensive wounds. Who hit my son in the head? Who killed my son? What about the fight at the party itself? Could that have been the source of the head wound? A head wound which was never even mentioned in the police autopsy, I might add." Mrs. Govindaiah appeared more disgusted with each contested fact she mentioned.

Growing increasingly more shrill, more out-of-control with each comment, Kiran's mother was led from the microphone in tears by her distressed husband.

A much calmer Lovely, Kiran's older sister, stepped to the microphone. "As you can see, my family is experiencing extreme stress and grief over the death of my younger brother. Please respect our privacy at this time. If you want to help us get to the bottom of the mystery of Kiran's death, we have established a website, www.JusticeforKiran.com. You can contribute to it. We will continue trying to find peace for Kiran and for ourselves."

Her remarks concluded, she walked to the doorway, where Officer Matthew Slade stood ready to escort her to his waiting police car.

One Year Later:

Chicago Tribune, February 12, 2015: "Officer Matthew Slade of the Carbondale Police Department was relieved of his duties on Friday, one year to the day after the disappearance of an SIU student that resulted in the student's death from hypothermia. Slade was charged with homicide in the death of Kiran Govindaiah.

Slade was the investigating officer during the February 12, 2014, search for Kiran Govindaiah, who froze to death in a field near Carbondale, Illinois, after disappearing from a nearby house party.

Slade's wife of six months, Lovely Govindaiah, is Kiran Govindaiah's older sister. It is believed that Kiran Govindaiah, the victim, opposed the marriage of the couple, and that may have led to his death on February 12th, 2013.

Theories are that Slade either found his brother-in-law unconscious and did not report his presence, which caused Govindaiah to freeze to death, or that he may have encountered him hitchhiking, an altercation ensued, and Officer Slade knocked him out and intentionally abandoned his body in the remote rural area.

The nineteen-year-old boy's body was discovered after six days of searching by volunteers. A truck driver Slade claims to have interviewed in the vicinity is asked to come forward if he remembers speaking with the officer that night."

◯

From the Author

For this third collection of stories that take the reader on a journey through the 9 Circles of Hell described in Dante's *Inferno*, I've drawn heavily from actual events and then fictionalized, as necessary. Only two stories of the nine are complete fabrications with no grounding in fact. Those two would be "The Monster Within" and "KILLAL."

Circle One: Limbo

The inspiration for "The Cave Robber" was a news item about the discovery of a brand-new species of spider, complete with a particularly creepy illustration. It was a short hop, skip and jump (pun intended) to the spelunking teenagers of this story.

Circle Two: Lust

"The Monster Within:" This is one of the few that did not stem from a news story, but, instead, from a writing prompt for a local "Iron Pen" competition, which gave the last line and asked the entrant to write to that line. (*I think my story "placed" in some way*). I re-used the Fort El Reno, Oklahoma setting from *Ghostly Tales of Route 66 (Vol. II)* and an actual tornado that touched down in that area recently provided creative fodder. As for the humanoid creatures,

New spider discovered in caves of Pacific Northwest

LOS ANGELES — They managed to avoid the notice of nosy humans beings for thousands of years, mostly by clinging to the roofs of dark caves and keeping their six, tiny eyes peeled for trouble.

But the secret existence of these eight-legged West Coasters has come to an end.

On Friday, scientists announced the discovery of a heretofore unknown family of spiders that some have playfully compared to Bigfoot, the privacy-loving man-beast of legend.

This undated photo from the California Academy of Sciences in San Francisco, shows a specimen of a new family of spiders, which scientists are calling Cave Robber (Trogloraptor marchingtoni) for its fearsome claws.

Associated Press

In the journal Zookeys, California Academy of Sciences arachnologist Charles E. Griswold and colleagues described their discovery of Trogloraptor, or "cave robber," a spider that is partial to caves and redwood debris in coastal forests from California to British Columbia.

Trogloraptor, which is roughly the size of a half-dollar coin when its legs are extended, has large raptorial claws, suggesting it is a fierce, specialized predator.

Roughly a dozen specimens were plucked from the roofs of caves by scientists and spelunkers who found them hanging from a few strands of spun silk.

The newly discovered arachnid is not about to give up all its long-held secrets, however. Scientists have yet to determine exactly how it mates, or what it eats. Captive Trogloraptors have so far refused to eat a variety of prey provided in the lab.

— Los Angeles Times

109

I've been watching the Steven Spielberg-produced "Extant" on television recently, but my story was written well before Halle Berry's creepy son, Ethan, graced the air waves. [Those readers who remember "MRM" from "Hellfire & Damnation II" will know that, like Mary Shelley, I'm interested in the idea of creating man, through cloning or any other method.]

Circle Three: Gluttony

Gluttony is always a difficult one to write. While we were touring New Zealand we visited The Elms. The story of "The Battle of Gate Pa" opened up infinite possibilities. Actually touring the site helped to anchor the story's location in my mind and researching the history behind the battle, I was fascinated by the idea that trench warfare originated there.

Circle Four: Avarice & Prodigality

"Boxed In" sprang from the real-life kidnapping of an heir to the Small Newspaper Group, Steven Small, which really occurred in 1987. Since my story has cicadas contributing to the eerie mood, I changed the time-line to 1986, but the kidnapping (and death) of the scion of a prominent Kankakee, Illinois, family was in the news again recently, as the female accomplice (*who went to jail for life*) was up for parole. The Chicago "Tribune" jogged my memory of the horrible story of Steven Small's kidnapping and how he was buried alive and died, after he was forced into a coffin-like box, held for ransom, and subsequently suffocated. Obviously, the ending of this story is different.

Circle Five: Wrath, Sullenness

"Do Not Go Gently" is the story of a dying man. I've now helped nurse four people through their final days, most recently my beloved mother-in-law, Helen Wilson, in February (2014). Neither my parents nor my husband's parents bore any resemblance at all to the sour hero of "Do Not Go Gently." They were all wonderful people who faced the end of their lives bravely and even with good humor. (*I remember my father telling a couple they had played bridge with for years, "I'll be getting to heaven before you. I'll get the cards ready."*) But the hospice literature and generally depressing nature of caring for a dying loved one, at home, for six months was fresh in my mind. It instantly took me back to caring for my father, who died in 1986 from terminal liver cancer, in a town so small that, to get the use of the ONE hospice room, you had to wait for the current occupant to die.

Circle Six: Heresy

"The Final Victim"—which probably seems very fanciful—is actually based on a case involving a Messianic figure who practiced witchcraft, lived in a trailer court across from the local high school and talked one of my former Silvis (IL) students into committing just such a murder of a man with a wooden leg. The birds as an "omen" may seem equally far-fetched, but the video I took of just such an occurrence can be seen on YouTube and on my blog, www.WeeklyWilson.com.

Circle Seven: The Violent

"KILLAL" arose from my one-time obsession with the phone game "Hanging with Friends." When I had an Android with a pull-out keyboard, I wasted hours playing this game. After I changed to an Apple IPhone, I no longer wanted to play it at all, as typing anything on the flat glass screen is not an easy task with my fingernails. This is one of the few stories that has no basis in fact. If you have never played "Hanging with Friends" it probably won't be your favorite, but I did enjoy the concept, and those of you who have ever played the game (or know of it) will be able to relate. I also liked the idea that both the main character (Alex) and the Flight Attendant (Allen) may end up dead in KILLAL.

Circle Eight: The Fraudulent

"The Mirror" arose from two news stories in the Midwest. First, there were "the boys in the bunkhouse" (as the workers in Atalissa, Iowa, were known). An actual documentary short was made about the shameful way in which these men of limited intelligence were victimized. All of the facts of their decades-long work for almost no pay are true. Only recently has "the bunkhouse" in Atalissa been torn down. The concept of the mirror from a hit-and-run death providing a clue to a killer occurred on Interstate 88 near Joslin on March 8, 2014. A 17-year old student from Villa Park, Emilio Perez, was struck by a hit-and-run driver after his car ran out of gas and he began walking on the shoulder of the highway for help. The driver did not stop. The mirror (and a few key pieces of the car that police did not release) was the only clue to the identity of the driver. Just yesterday (September 5th, 2014) a Crime Stoppers tip (*and, possibly, the $10,000 reward that went with it*) led to the apprehension of a female driver, Maria E. Romero, age 41, of Rockford, Illinois, who was charged with leaving the scene of a fatal accident and failing to report an accident causing a death (Class 4 and Class 1 felonies). The accused cannot bond out of the Rock Island County Jail because the United States Immigration and Customs Enforcement Service has determined that Romero is an illegal alien and they are seeking to deport her. Should she go to trial in the United States, she faced a penalty of one to three years in prison. The story detail about a deer running into my car actually happened to me during the 2004 presidential caucuses in Iowa, when I was driving I-380 between Iowa City and Cedar Rapids, Iowa, on my way to Waterloo/Cedar Falls for a John Kerry rally.

Circle Nine: Treachery

"A Losing Hand" was inspired by the real-life death of a Southern Illinois University student who froze to death. The names, of course, are all fictional. The story events are not based on fact, although the death of the victim was the original starting point. This story is still not resolved. Many of the reactions by family members *did* occur as I have described them, with the family demanding an independent autopsy, etc. It has not (yet) been resolved to the satisfaction of the grieving relatives of the Indian youth.

There is no similarity to real-life events or people, beyond the initial inspiration to take the outcome and speculate; just the incident, itself, reported online or in print, would set off a creative spark that led somewhere very different. Nevertheless, there are events occurring like those I have described every day of the week. Some speak to me more than others.

I hope you enjoy the collection. If you do, I hope you will consider reading the first two books in the series, *Hellfire & Damnation* (the first book) and *Hellfire & Damnation II*. You can revisit those first two books at www. HellfireAndDamnationTheBook.com and leaving reviews on Amazon and Goodreads is always greatly appreciated.

You can also contact me at my website, www.ConnieCWilson.com.

Thank you, in advance, for your interest in my writing.

– Connie (Corcoran) Wilson
September 6, 2014

Also by Connie Corcoran Wilson...

"*Hellfire & Damnation* is an impressive collection, a series of remarkable tales—some based on true stories—organized around a brilliant and unifying theme that echoes Dante's *Inferno*: Wilson's harrowing work will stay with you long after you finish the final page."

– Lisa Mannetti,
The Gentling Box

"Connie (Corcoran) Wilson's *Hellfire & Damnation II* is a remarkable collection of somber, noirish, flat-out scary and altogether satisfying stories that seek to find hope in a dark world that defies it. Her subtle irony and penchant for finding terror in the least expected places will generate comparisons to Stephen King and Ray Bradbury, with just a hint of Philip K. Dick thrown in. Wilson has a wondrous voice.

– Jon Land,
author of the Caitlin Stong series

HellfireAndDamnationTheBook.com

For more information, visit:

www.HellfireAndDamnationTheBook.com

and

www.ConnieCWilson.com